DOUBLE LOVE

Elizabeth ran down the last flight of stairs, tore through the lobby, and rushed toward the big Romanesque clock that was the pride of Sweet Valley High.

Please, Todd, don't be angry with me for being late, she prayed silently. If only he wanted to ask her to the dance, it would be all right. She would forgive Jessica for everything.

At first she didn't see Todd. But then, as she came outside, there he was—walking across the lawn to the little red Spider and climbing in beside Jessica. Her own twin sister!

Bantam Books in the Sweet Valley High Series
Ask your bookseller for the books you have missed

#1 DOUBLE LOVE
#2 SECRETS
#3 PLAYING WITH FIRE
#4 POWER PLAY
#5 ALL NIGHT LONG
#6 DANGEROUS LOVE
#7 DEAR SISTER
#8 HEARTBREAKER
#9 RACING HEARTS
#10 WRONG KIND OF GIRL
#11 TOO GOOD TO BE TRUE
#12 WHEN LOVE DIES
#13 KIDNAPPED!
#14 DECEPTIONS
#15 PROMISES
#16 RAGS TO RICHES
#17 LOVE LETTERS
#18 HEAD OVER HEELS
#19 SHOWDOWN
#20 CRASH LANDING!
#21 RUNAWAY
#22 TOO MUCH IN LOVE
#23 SAY GOODBYE
#24 MEMORIES
#25 NOWHERE TO RUN
#26 HOSTAGE!
#27 LOVESTRUCK
#28 ALONE IN THE CROWD
#29 BITTER RIVAL
#30 JEALOUS LIES
#31 TAKING SIDES
#32 THE NEW JESSICA

Super Edition: PERFECT SUMMER
Super Edition: SPECIAL CHRISTMAS
Super Edition: SPRING BREAK
Super Edition: MALIBU SUMMER

SWEET VALLEY HIGH

DOUBLE LOVE

Written by
Kate William

Created by
FRANCINE PASCAL

BANTAM BOOKS
TORONTO • NEW YORK • LONDON • SYDNEY • AUCKLAND

RL 5, IL age 12 and up

DOUBLE LOVE
A Bantam Book / October 1983
10 printings through April 1986

Sweet Valley High is a trademark of Francine Pascal

Conceived by Francine Pascal

Produced by Cloverdale Press, Inc.

Cover art by James Mathewuse

ISBN 0-553-25033-7

Published simultaneously in the United States and Canada

PRINTED IN THE UNITED STATES OF AMERICA

O   19   18   17   16

One

"Oh, Lizzie, do you believe how absolutely horrendous I look today!" Jessica Wakefield groaned as she stepped in front of her sister, Elizabeth, and stared at herself in the bedroom mirror. "I'm so gross! Just look at me. Everything is totally wrong. To begin with, I'm disgustingly fat. . . ." With that, she spun around to show off a stunning figure without an extra ounce visible anywhere.

She moaned again, this time holding out one perfectly shaped bronze leg. "Isn't that the grossest? I swear I must have the skinniest legs in America. And the bumpiest knees. What am I going to do? How can I possibly go to school looking like this today? Today of all days!"

Jessica, stared at herself in the full-length mirror and saw a picture of utter heartbreak and despair. But what was actually reflected in the glass was about the most adorable, most dazzling sixteen-year-old girl imaginable. Yet there was no stopping Jessica Wakefield when she was in this mood.

"Why couldn't I at least have had an oval face? It looks like someone stuck a pumpkin on top of my neck. And this hair—a dull yellow mess of split ends. I hate it!"

In a gesture of absolute hopelessness, she ran her hand under her silky blond hair, flipped it up, and watched as it drifted lightly back to her shoulders.

"Only thing duller are my eyes. Look at that color, Liz." She poked her face an inch from her sister's nose and fluttered long eyelashes over almond-shaped eyes the blue-green of the Caribbean. "They're so blah."

Without waiting for Elizabeth's response, Jessica reached again into her bag of sorrows. "I mean, there could be a telethon just for all the things that're wrong with me! I can't even look at myself another minute!" And with that she threw herself facedown on her sister's freshly made bed.

"Thanks a million," Elizabeth said in mock anger.

"I wasn't talking about you," came Jessica's pillow-muffled voice.

"Oh, no? All you said was that you're the

grossest-looking person in all of Sweet Valley. Your figure's terrible, your legs are chopsticks, your knees are bony, and on top of that, your face is all wrong. Right?''

''Right.''

''And I just happen to be your identical twin sister. So what does that make me—Miss America?'' Elizabeth asked, deciding to take a good look in the mirror. If Jessica were such a hopeless case, she might be in trouble, too. But the image she saw reflected in the mirror was hardly cause for alarm.

Both girls had the same shoulder-length, sun-streaked blond hair, the same sparkling blue-green eyes, the same perfect skin. Even the tiny dimple in Elizabeth's left cheek was duplicated in her younger sister's—younger by four minutes. Both girls were five feet six on the button and generously blessed with spectacular, all-American good looks. Both wore exactly the same size clothes, but they refused to dress alike, except for the exquisite identical lavalieres they wore on gold chains around their necks. The lavalieres had been presents from their parents on their sixteenth birthday.

The only way you could tell them apart was by the tiny beauty mark on Elizabeth's right shoulder. Their friends might notice that Elizabeth wore a watch and that Jessica did not. Time was never a problem for Jessica. She always felt that things didn't really start until she got there. And if she was late, let 'em wait. Otherwise, there was virtually no way to distinguish between the beautiful Wakefield twins. But beneath the skin, there was a world of difference. A wicked gleam of mischief lurked in the aquamarine depths of Jessica's eyes, while Elizabeth's reflected only sincerity.

When the phone in the hallway shrilled, Jessica leaped to answer it, assuming, of course, that it was for her.

"Jessica? Liz?" a boy's voice asked.

"Jessica, of course! And who's this?" she demanded.

"Oh, hi, Jessica. This is Todd. Todd Wilkins. Is Liz home?"

He wanted her sister! Jessica's eyes narrowed dangerously. One of the cutest boys at Sweet Valley High, and he was calling to talk to Elizabeth! Todd Wilkins was currently the basketball team's hottest star, and Jessica had been admiring him for some time now as she practiced her cheers in the gym alongside him. The idea that he would prefer Elizabeth to her infuriated Jessica, though she was extra careful to conceal this from him.

"Todd," she purred, "I should have known it was you just from your voice. I'm so glad you called. You know, I've been meaning to tell you—that was an absolutely fantastic drive shot

4

you made during practice today. I was really impressed."

"Uh, gee, Jessica—thanks." She could almost hear Todd blushing. "I didn't know you were watching."

"I *always* make it a point to watch the best players." *And the best-looking players*, she added silently. "You know, you could probably play professionally one of these days if you really wanted to, Todd." Jessica heaped on the flattery, hoping to distract him from the real purpose of his call.

But Todd hadn't forgotten. "That's really nice of you to say so, but it's probably too soon to tell." He paused. "Listen, Jessica, it's been nice talking to you, but is Liz around?"

Jessica frowned. "Uh, I think she's in the shower."

"I could wait," Todd said hopefully.

"Oh, you wouldn't want to do that. Liz stays in the shower practically *forever*."

"Maybe I should try calling back in a few minutes." His disappointment was evident.

"You could, but she probably won't be here. We've got to run, or we'll be late for school. This is the big day—they're announcing the Pi Beta pledges! Liz and I will just die if we don't get in!"

"I'm sure you won't have any trouble," said Todd. "But good luck anyway."

Jessica experienced a slight twinge of guilt about sidetracking Todd, but she quickly brushed it away, telling herself she really hadn't done any harm. It wasn't as if he were Elizabeth's boyfriend. She probably didn't even know he existed.

Jessica couldn't have been more mistaken. Just as she was hanging up, Elizabeth poked her head around the doorway. "Who was that?" she asked.

"Oh, just Todd Wilkins," Jessica replied, flashing her sister a brilliant smile to cover up the deception. "He called to wish me good luck with Pi Beta today. Wasn't that sweet of him?"

Elizabeth's heart sank, but she didn't let Jessica see her disappointment. She'd been hoping Todd would call her. The other day she'd caught him glancing at her in the cafeteria line. She'd turned around and there he was—tall, lean, his gorgeous brown eyes looking straight at her. She had quickly glanced down at her tray, a blush coloring her cheeks. Had Todd realized how much she liked him? He sat near her in Mr. Russo's science class, and though she'd never spoken to him, she'd always been aware of his compelling presence. In the cafeteria she had cast another glance over her shoulder. As their eyes met again, they both smiled. Elizabeth felt as if she'd been jolted by a thousand watts of electricity.

He was waiting for her after school that day. As she caught sight of him, leaning against the front railing, his sky-blue shirt open at the throat to reveal a glimpse of tanned, muscular chest, Elizabeth's pulse took off at a gallop. As he caught sight of her, a slow, shy smile spread across his features. He was nervous, too, she realized.

"Hey, Liz, I—I was wondering if you had today's chem assignment. I forgot to copy it down."

"Chemistry assignment?" Elizabeth couldn't tear her eyes off that blinding white smile. "Uh, sure, I think I have it somewhere. . . ."

Frantically, she began juggling books, searching for the assignment she'd scribbled hastily on a sheet of loose-leaf paper.

"Are you always this organized?" Todd teased, his coffee-colored eyes dancing.

"Only when it comes to chemistry." She laughed, thinking of the special chemistry between Todd and her and hoping he wouldn't notice how nervous he made her.

She walked away from Todd that day, feeling as if she were floating two feet off the pavement.

Now, discovering that Todd had preferred Jessica all along, Elizabeth felt as if she'd been grounded by a five-hundred-pound weight. Not wanting to reveal her true feelings about Todd, she quickly changed the subject.

7

"Speaking of Pi Beta," she said, "have you decided what you're going to wear today?"

At noon the Wakefield twins would find out if they had made Pi Beta Alpha, "the positively best sorority at Sweet Valley High," according to Jessica. That meant "the snobbiest" in Elizabeth's book.

"Wear?" squealed Jessica, her thoughts immediately switching from Todd back to the subject of her hideous appearance. "I have nothing, absolutely nothing to wear."

"This sounds like a job for my new tuxedo shirt," Elizabeth offered. She'd thought about wearing it herself, hoping to impress Todd when she saw him, but suddenly it didn't seem to matter.

"Nothing will help." Jessica moaned.

Elizabeth shrugged. "Well, it was just a thought." She began collecting the books she'd need for school.

"But it's a beginning," Jessica said quickly. "Could I wear the pants, too?"

"I think I've been had."

"And the little bow tie?"

"On one condition," Elizabeth said. "I want the whole outfit back, clean and hanging in my closet, by the weekend."

"On my honor."

Elizabeth groaned. "I'm doomed."

"Elizabeth Wakefield, you're the best!" Jessica headed for Elizabeth's closet. "At least now I won't have to look totally gross on the most important day of my life."

"Come on, Jess," Elizabeth argued. "Getting into Pi Beta isn't *that* big a deal. In fact, I'm beginning to wonder if I ever should have let you talk me into pledging."

"How can you say that?" Jessica shrieked. "You know how important a sorority is. Especially this one. All the top people are in it."

"You mean all the snootiest."

It was an echo of the argument they'd had two weeks earlier when Jessica had pleaded with her sister to pledge. Eventually Elizabeth had given in. Mostly because she and Jessica always did things together, and she didn't want anything as dumb as a sorority to come between them.

Jessica had assured Elizabeth that the pledge dares they'd be required to do would be nothing major. "Just a lot of silly fun!" she'd insisted.

Fun! Their first dare had been to order a pepperoni pizza from Guido's Pizza Palace, to be delivered during Mr. Russo's chemistry class.

"I'll die!" Elizabeth had protested. Just the thought of Mr. Russo's reaction petrified her. Bob Russo was the most brilliant—and most demanding—teacher at Sweet Valley. He was highly temperamental, with a biting sense of humor. You never knew when he would cut

9

you down or stare you into a tiny, shrinking smudge for saying something stupid. Every kid at school was terrified of him. And now they were going to have a pizza . . .

"It'll be a scream," Jessica had said.

It had been a scream, all right. A delivery man wearing stereo headphones and a tomato-stained apron had walked right into the classroom carrying a humungous, steaming, smelly pepperoni pizza and stood there looking questioningly as Mr. Russo was writing a complicated formula on the blackboard.

"Yes?"

"Your pizza?" the delivery man had asked, and the class had gone into collective cardiac arrest. Somebody snorted, trying to stifle a laugh. Somebody else giggled. Elizabeth's face turned the color of the tomato stains on the delivery man's apron.

"Pardon me?" Mr. Russo asked innocently, still preoccupied with the lesson. That did it. The entire class cracked up and howled with laughter.

"One double pepperoni pizza for"—the delivery man examined his order form—"Elizabeth Wakefield."

Elizabeth's face was on fire. Everybody looked around at her in disbelief. Elizabeth Wakefield—the level-headed, serious twin—had flipped out!

Only Elizabeth knew who had really ordered the pizza—and given her name.

"Well, well," said Mr. Russo. "Elizabeth, is this by any chance a science project?" More laughter from the kids.

Elizabeth panicked. *What will I say?* Shooting a glance at Jessica, she knew instantly she was on her own. Her twin wore the angelic expression of a totally innocent bystander.

"Uh—yes, sir," Elizabeth stammered, groping for a way out. "Uh—see—we wondered how much heat the pizza would lose getting from the pizza parlor to here—and uh . . ."

Even Mr. Russo had to smile. He rummaged through a desk drawer and produced a thermometer. "I see," he said. "Well, then, let's take the pizza's temperature, before it undergoes a chemical change—commonly called digestion."

So they had gotten away with that pledge dare. They'd survived the other crazy pranks, too. Second on the list was delivering the singing telegram to Chrome Dome—Mr. Cooper, Sweet Valley High's somewhat stuffy principal. Finally, they'd grossed out the entire cafeteria by dyeing the mashed potatoes purple.

And now the big day had arrived. At noon they would find out if they were in Pi Beta. Elizabeth wasn't too excited about it, but Jessica had the date circled in red on her calendar. Nothing could spoil this day for her—except of course, not getting into the sorority, which wasn't a likely possibility.

For Elizabeth, the day was already spoiled. As she thought of Todd's phone call to Jessica, the tight feeling in her chest spread to a pressure behind her eyes. But she was determined not to let Jessica know how she felt about Todd. What was the point? It was obvious which sister Todd preferred. And why not? What girl could possibly compete with the dazzling Jessica Wakefield?

Two

Jessica was already at the breakfast table when Elizabeth sat down.

"Your father's going to be working late again tonight," Alice Wakefield told her daughters as she served french toast.

"What's up, Dad? A merger? A war between two giant conglomerates?" asked Jessica, bringing a smile to her father's face. Ned Wakefield was always a pushover for his lively daughters.

"Both—and then some," he said. "Big doings. There may be serious consequences for the Sweet Valley High football team. The playing field is becoming a battlefield."

"Really? What's going on?" Elizabeth asked.

"As a lawyer on the case, I can't tell you. It's too soon and too complicated," her father said. "Marianna and I are working on it. I will be late

13

again, though. Isn't that enough bad news for you?"

"OK, mystery man." Jessica laughed.

"Jessica," said her mother, "aren't you coming home late, too? Don't you have cheerleading practice?"

"Right, I won't be home till at least seven."

"And, Liz, isn't this a late afternoon for you at *The Oracle?*"

"Uh-huh. Looks like the whole Wakefield clan will be out doing things," Elizabeth said.

"Therefore . . ." said Alice Wakefield.

Elizabeth and Jessica knew what was coming.

"Therefore—you can drive the Fiat today," she said.

The twins squealed with delight. Only on rare occasions were they allowed to drive to school in the family's second car, a little red Spider convertible.

"Oh, wow," Jessica said, jumping up. "Am I going to be hot today! In my tuxedo shirt, driving my Fiat! Look out, Sweet Valley!"

"Jessica," her mother interrupted, "I'm sorry, honey, but Liz will have to drive."

"What?" Jessica's anguished wail filled the entire kitchen of the Wakefield's split-level home.

"Jessica, you know very well that you can't drive for three weeks. And you can stop looking at me that way. *You're* the one who had the accident."

"That's not fair!" Jessica whined. "I'm not going to school to be humiliated like a kindergarten child! Oh, forget it, Mom, just forget it. I know Liz is your favorite, and I'm just an afterthought!"

"Come on, Jess, let's get going," Elizabeth said patiently. "You know you're not going to miss today for the world. What's Pi Beta Alpha going to do without *you*? Let's just go, or we'll be late for school."

"Accident!" Jessica muttered after they had climbed into the car and were driving through Sweet Valley, the little green jewel of a California town where they lived.

"It was just a tiny dent in the fender. She makes it sound like a six-car pileup on the L.A. freeway!"

"That *tiny dent* cost two hundred dollars to fix," Elizabeth said dryly, wishing her sister would stop complaining and let her enjoy the drive through the valley. As she did very often, Elizabeth thought how lucky she and Jessica were to live in Sweet Valley. Everything about it was terrific—the gently rolling hills, the quaint downtown area, and the fantastic white sand beach only fifteen minutes away. She and Jessica were even luckier now, with a new in-ground pool in the backyard.

15

"Don't you wish we lived up here on the hill like the Patmans and the Fowlers?"

"You can't be serious, Jess," Elizabeth admonished. But she knew perfectly well that her twin was totally serious about wanting to live on the hill where Sweet Valley's very rich lived in sprawling, imposing mansions. "Dad does all right," Elizabeth went on. "He certainly works hard enough. He's out late practically every night these days."

"Lizzie, I've been wondering about that. Does that seem funny?"

"What?"

"Dad out every night. And one night I called his office, and that new woman lawyer answered."

"You mean Ms. West?"

"Yes. But you heard what Dad called her this morning—*Marianna!*"

"Well, that's her name, silly," said Elizabeth, trying to sound more unconcerned than she really was. She had wondered about her father and Marianna, too.

"Well, I don't know, Liz. She sounded pretty seductive on the phone."

"Jessica, really! Sometimes I think you're wacko!"

"OK, OK, don't get so shook, Liz." Jessica glanced out at the spacious homes and heaved a great sigh. "Anyway, I'm not saying I don't like our house, Liz. But having a lot of money, like Bruce Patman and Lila Fowler, can't be all bad."

"And what about what goes with it?" asked Elizabeth.

"You mean all those cars and servants?"

"C'mon, Jess, you know what I'm talking about. This crazy feud—the Patmans want every rock in Sweet Valley to stay exactly where it's been for fifty years, and the Fowlers want to build over everything in sight. Who needs that?"

Jessica changed the subject with her usual abruptness as the school came into view. "Oh, Liz, please stop and let me drive into the parking lot," she pleaded.

"Jess, you heard what Mom said."

Jessica sank into her seat. "You heard what Mom said," she mimicked nastily. "Sometimes I wonder how anybody so wimpy can be my sister."

Elizabeth slid the Fiat into an empty space in the student parking lot. "Come on, Jess, what difference does it make?"

"None, of course, Aunt Fanny!"

Elizabeth sighed. She knew that tone all too well. It meant a storm was brewing, one that could turn into Hurricane Jessica.

"I'm sure you'll be allowed to drive again soon," she said encouragingly.

But Jessica wasn't listening to a word. She

17

was out of the car in a flash, slamming the door so hard that Elizabeth winced. How did it always turn out this way? She just did what her mother said, and somehow she was always wrong. Even worse, she felt guilty.

"Jess, please!" Elizabeth said, scrambling out of the car and facing her stormy-eyed twin. Jessica just stood there smoldering, refusing to relent.

"Look, I'll talk to Mom for you," Elizabeth said. "I'll ask her to let you drive tomorrow."

"Tomorrow!" Jessica sneered. "You may be a tomorrow person. *I* am a today person. Don't do me any favors."

Jessica wasn't going to let up. She kept turning away, refusing to look at Elizabeth. Jessica could hold a grudge the way the Patmans held on to their money—forever!

Just as Elizabeth was deciding this was a lost cause, she saw Enid Rollins, her best friend, coming across the lawn, waving to her. Something was cooking with Enid. She had sounded excited when she called Elizabeth the night before and said she had something "vital" to tell her. Elizabeth was dying to find out, but Jessica was still pouting.

"Jess, I have to talk to Enid."

"How can you be best friends with somebody as blah as Eeny Rollins? I don't want you to go over there. Somebody might think it was *me* talking to her."

"Enid is a wonderful person. Why don't you like her?"

"Eeny is a nerd. And there's something weird about her."

Just then Jessica glanced over her shoulder. Apparently something she saw swept away her anger in a flash. She threw her arms around Elizabeth and gave her a swift, powerful hug, almost lifting her off the ground.

"I've decided to forgive you," she announced, beaming. "Go on, talk to Enid. I'll see you at noon."

Surprised, but not unaccustomed to Jessica's swift changes of mood, Elizabeth hugged her back and ran to catch up with Enid.

"So what's the big news?" Elizabeth asked as she fell in step with her friend.

"Shhhhhhhhh! Not so loud, Liz," Enid Rollins said, looking around and blushing, as though the entire student body were eavesdropping.

Elizabeth smiled. "Don't be silly. There's nobody near us."

When Enid didn't smile back, Elizabeth knew her friend had something serious to discuss. Elizabeth and Enid had become best friends when they had taken a creative writing class together the year before. Enid was a terrific person, Elizabeth thought, and absolutely *not* a nerd, no matter what Jessica said. With her shoulder-length brown hair and large green eyes, she was really pretty. And in her quiet way, she was very smart—and very funny. Jessica figured anyone who was quiet was dull, but Enid Rollins was anything but dull. There was something almost mysterious about her, as though she knew things that other people didn't, or had a secret she wanted to keep.

They were nearing the school door when Elizabeth saw handsome, spoiled Bruce Patman sliding his black Porsche into a parking spot. Enid tugged on her friend's arm.

"Let's sit a second," she said.

Elizabeth quickly sat down beside her on the grass, eager for the news. "Well?"

Enid blushed even redder than before. Then she smiled so radiantly that for a moment she became a brand-new person.

"Who is he?" Elizabeth asked.

"What?" Enid looked shocked.

"You heard me. Who is he?"

Enid shook her head in amazement. "How can you see into people like that, Liz? You could be a detective—or even a mystery writer."

Now it was Elizabeth's turn to blush. Enid knew her secret dream—to be a writer. Not just a reporter, the way she was on *The Oracle*, but a serious writer. Someday she wanted to write poems or plays or even novels. She was sharpening her skills, too, right now at the school newspaper. Elizabeth wrote the "Eyes and Ears" column for *The Oracle*, but no one knew who the writer of the column was—and Elizabeth couldn't even tell her best friend about it. Many times she ached to tell Enid or Jessica or *somebody*—but she didn't. Only Mr. Collins, the faculty adviser for the paper, knew.

It was a tradition at Sweet Valley that if the identity of the writer of the "Eyes and Ears" column was discovered before the end of the term, the students threw that person fully clothed into the swimming pool. Elizabeth Wakefield had no intention of being unmasked.

Now Elizabeth searched Enid's flushed face, wondering if Enid had figured out her big secret. But, no—Enid's mind was occupied with something entirely different.

"Guess who called me?" she finally blurted out.

"Who? Tell me!"

"Ronnie Edwards, the new guy in Miss Markey's class. I noticed him looking at me in the cafeteria the other day," Enid said dreamily.

"But he's so quiet. He never says a word!"

"You have to get to know him," Enid explained. "Some people need more time to open up, you know."

"Oh, yes, I know." Enid could have been describing herself, Elizabeth thought. It had taken a long time to really get to know Enid, but it was worth it.

"So—what did he call about?"

"He asked me to the Phi Epsilon dance!"

"Oh, Enid, that's wonderful!"

"Isn't it great! I'm so happy!" Enid said. Then she asked quietly, "Who are you going with?"

"Well, I don't know."

"Don't worry. He'll ask you," Enid said.

"Who will?"

"You know."

That's why Enid Rollins was such a good friend. She knew exactly how to say something without really saying it. Enid was aware of Elizabeth's crush on Todd, but she was too nice to mention him by name when things were not settled yet.

Elizabeth was getting ready to dig for more news about Ronnie and Enid when Enid's eyes went wild and she pulled Elizabeth back.

"Look out! That maniac!" Enid screamed as she and Elizabeth tumbled over on the grass.

Elizabeth looked up in confusion, trying to figure out what was happening. She saw a red blur zip past them up the long school driveway. Then a little red car screeched to a rather spectacular stop next to Bruce Patman's black Porsche.

Jessica!

Elizabeth gave a quick look at the parking

spot where she had left the Fiat. She didn't see it. Then she shoved her hand into her pocket to feel the car keys. They were gone! And then she remembered Jessica's sudden hug—that was when she had filched the keys.

"I'll see you at noon, Enid," Elizabeth said angrily. "I've got to talk to my darling little sister!"

"OK. But don't tell anybody about—"

"Don't worry."

Elizabeth marched toward the black Porsche and the red Fiat. There sat tall, handsome, dark-haired Bruce Patman, lounging arrogantly behind the wheel of his flashy sports car. And there stood Jessica, acting as if absolutely nothing had happened.

This time I'm really going to let her have it, Elizabeth fumed to herself as she ran toward her sister. She was so angry that she didn't even notice somebody running alongside her.

"Hey, what's the hurry?" It was Todd Wilkins, and he was smiling. "I was hoping to talk to you."

Elizabeth was in total shock. There he was— Todd Wilkins—the man of her dreams, standing two inches away from her.

"Oh—uh, well," she stammered. "What about?" She could have kicked herself. Why did she turn into a complete idiot the minute Todd was near her?

"Said like an ace reporter." Todd laughed. "Right to the point. Lois Lane had better watch out for you."

They were both laughing now. Then Todd said, "I was wondering if—"

Just then the bell rang, and students started swarming toward the building.

Todd frowned. "We'll be late," he muttered. "Listen, will you be around after basketball practice?"

"Sure," Elizabeth said, her heart beating faster. "I have to stay late at *The Oracle*. How about under the clock—around five-fifteen?"

"I'll be there."

Elizabeth watched starry-eyed as Todd loped gracefully across the lawn. Suddenly she remembered Jessica! She whirled around and spotted the black Porsche and the red Fiat. Jessica was gone.

Between classes, the halls of Sweet Valley High resembled the battle scene from *Star Wars*, with bodies hurtling in all directions accompanied by collisions and dropped books. It was while Elizabeth was picking up hers that Jessica raced by, wearing a smile brighter than California sunshine in July.

"I have the most sensational news, Liz!"

Down on her hands and knees, Elizabeth

looked up. Why, she wondered, didn't Jessica ever get caught in such ungraceful situations? Because she was Jessica. If a book of hers ever fell, there was always a handy male eager to pick it up.

"What news, Jess?"

"You won't believe it."

"Is it about the dance?"

"You'll see." And she darted off, pausing to look back. "Lizzie, dear, do get up off the floor. I would positively die if anyone thought it was me grubbing around like that."

Bite your tongue, Elizabeth warned herself. *Don't say what you're thinking. Murder's still illegal in California!*

She gathered her books and stood up. It wasn't until she was halfway down the hall that she realized she'd been so angry at Jessica's remark that she had forgotten to ask for the car keys!

At noon, just as the president of Pi Beta Alpha was about to announce the list of new sorority members, Jessica leaned over to Elizabeth and whispered, "I think Todd's going to ask me to the Phi Epsilon dance."

Elizabeth felt as if a balloon had just burst inside her. Tears welled up in her eyes.

"Elizabeth Wakefield, congratulations!" the

president shouted. "Elizabeth, where are you? Come up here and join your sisters."

Heads turned to look at her. Everyone thought she was crying with happiness. Somehow she made herself stand up, but she couldn't make herself look at Jessica. She would never tell Jessica now how she felt about Todd. And she would never, *ever* stand in Jessica's way—but she couldn't look at her sister just then.

Jessica was tugging on her sleeve, trying to stop her as she was about to make her way to the front of the room.

"What about me?" Jessica hissed. "Why haven't they called *my* name?"

The president called out, "Cara Walker, congratulations!" Jessica applauded reluctantly for her friend.

Elizabeth stood beside Jessica's seat. She wouldn't go up there and accept membership until Jessica's name was called. After all, the only reason she had decided to pledge Pi Beta was so she and Jessica would be together.

Lila Fowler, another friend of Jessica's, was called. Even Enid Rollins got in, and she'd pledged Pi Beta mainly to keep Elizabeth company. Elizabeth applauded loudly for her best friend. But still Jessica's name was not called. Could it be that her sister might have been blackballed? Jessica, co-captain of the cheerleaders, beautiful, popular Jessica?

With a pleased smile, the president announced, "Last but absolutely not least—Jessica Wakefield, congratulations!"

Elizabeth and Jessica ran up to the front of the room. Even though her tears had dried, Elizabeth felt as if she were still sobbing on the inside.

Jessica was ecstatic. "There's so much I want to learn about Pi Beta Alpha," she was gushing to one of the senior girls. "For instance, just how many votes do you need to become president?"

For Elizabeth, the rest of the day was spent playing catch-up, but she never quite did. She was late getting to the newspaper office, late getting the column finished, and late going over it with Mr. Collins. Didn't it always happen that way when you had someplace special to go? she wondered. Todd was probably waiting for her under the clock right now. What did he want to talk about?

Please don't be angry with me for being late, she prayed silently. If only Todd wanted to ask her to the dance, it would be all right. She would forgive Jessica for everything—even for swiping the car keys.

Elizabeth ran down the last flight of stairs, tore through the lobby, and rushed toward the big Romanesque clock that was the pride of Sweet Valley High.

At first she didn't see Todd. But then, as she came outside, there he was—walking across the lawn to their little red Spider and climbing in beside Jessica!

Elizabeth's heart sank. She stood there, numb with shock, as the convertible backed up and spun merrily down the drive, carrying Jessica and Todd.

Three

"Hey, is anybody home?" The call brought Elizabeth to the top of the stairs.

"Steven!"

"You must be that ugly Wakefield twin I hear so much about. What's the matter? No hello for your older and infinitely wiser brother?"

Elizabeth hurtled down the stairs and into her brother's outstretched arms.

"Your repulsive face couldn't have shown up at a better time," she said with her first real laugh all day.

Disentangling himself from his sister's hug, Steven gave her a questioning look. "Yeah? What's up?"

"Oh, nothing," she lied hastily. "I just have these spells when I get totally weird—and actually start missing *you*."

"Sure you do. I'm repulsive but lovable. So tell me, how many princes did you turn into toads this week?"

Elizabeth pretended to think for a moment, then held up six fingers and shrugged. "Slow week. Seems fewer and fewer princes are passing through Sweet Valley these days. But I bet you have no trouble stopping clocks at State U. with that face of yours."

"You know it. When I get through with that place, no one will know what time it is."

Sister and brother stood smiling at each other, enjoying the special bond they shared. Elizabeth's blond beauty came from their mother, while Steven's dark good looks made him a younger version of Ned Wakefield. Slightly over six feet tall with beautiful brown eyes and a slim, athletic build, Steven had long been a target of crushes from Elizabeth and Jessica's girlfriends.

The two had started their "ugly" routine ages ago after spending a totally boring afternoon listening to a distant relative drone on and on about "how too, too adorable you children are. Just too, too!" They had invited Jessica to join in their game, but she was never bored when people discussed her beauty.

"Tell you what, little sister," Steven said now. "I'm starving. If you *insist* on fixing me something, I promise not to complain about your cooking."

"Insist! How do you know I don't have ten more important things to do?"

She couldn't resist the mock hangdog look on her brother's face. "OK, I insist, I insist! Let's go check the fridge for possibilities."

While Steven made himself comfortable at the round kitchen table, Elizabeth checked out the contents of the large, copper-colored refrigerator.

"How are things on the home front these days?" he asked.

"Oh, great, just great," Elizabeth mumbled, her back to him.

"What?"

Carrying cold cuts, mustard, pickles, and a carton of milk, she came over to the table. "Things are OK. The usual, I guess. School, homework. Stuff—you know."

Should she tell Steven about Todd? she asked herself. Or about Jessica? Or about Jessica *and* Todd, hating to link those two names even in her mind. No, she decided. It wouldn't be fair to put Steven in the middle.

"Stuff? You might not be much to look at, but I always thought you knew how to talk," Steven teased.

"One more crack out of you, Steven Wakefield, and I'll fix you a knuckle sandwich!"

"Peace!" he said, throwing up his arms in surrender. He grew serious as he watched Elizabeth fix him a huge sandwich.

"You know, Lizzie, big brothers are great listeners."

She smiled at his concern.

"Steve, things are fine. Just fine!" *Or they will be when I'm dead and can't think of Todd anymore,* she added to herself. "And now if you're through grilling me, big brother, how about telling me why you're home for the fourth weekend in a row. I thought sophisticated college men spent their weekends dating sophisticated college women."

"Well, you know, I, uh, like to see the family once in a while." Elizabeth could have sworn he was blushing.

"Sure you do, Steve. And we're really grateful for the fifteen minutes you spend with us every weekend. What I'm absolutely dying to know is where you spend the rest of the time."

"I see old friends. That kind of thing." Then he laughed. "You're getting to be a nosy brat, you know that?"

"OK," she relented. "I'll let you off the hook for now, but I'm not through with you yet. I sense a mystery here, and you know how I love a mystery."

"Nosy *and* weird—what a combination," he said, biting into his sandwich. "Tell me what's new with Jessica and the folks."

"Jess is fine." *Boy, is she ever,* Elizabeth thought. "And the folks are, too, I guess."

"You guess?" he asked between bites.

"They're so busy I hardly see them. Mom's always rushing off to meet a client. Her design business is really booming. And Dad—well, he's always out. He's working on a case with a new lawyer in the firm, somebody by the name of Marianna West. She used to be married to that big heart specialist, Gareth West."

"Dad and a divorcée? Hmmm." Steven lifted one eyebrow.

"For heaven's sake, Steve, you're as bad as Jessica. She said, and I quote, 'If I were married, I wouldn't let my husband spend so much time with a good-looking divorcée!' "

Steven nearly choked on his sandwich at Elizabeth's perfect imitation of their sister's voice.

"If I know Jess, she wouldn't let a husband of hers get any farther from her than the length of a two-foot leash," he said.

Just then the back door flew open, and Jessica whirled in, smiling as only she could when her day had been a perfect dream.

"Steve!" she squealed, dropping her books on the counter and rushing to hug her brother. "I didn't know you were coming this weekend!" She stepped back to get a better look at him.

"You're absolutely too gorgeous! Aren't we lucky, Lizzie?" she asked, turning to flash dazzling white teeth at her unsmiling sister. "We probably have the town's—maybe even the state's—handsomest brother!"

"What, that repulsive thing?" Elizabeth teased.

"What, this repulsive thing?" Steven added.

"Why in the world are you two still playing that ridiculous game? You wouldn't think it was funny if you really were gross-looking," Jessica said, shuddering at the thought of having anything other than an attractive family.

Elizabeth busied herself with cleaning up the table, tuning out Jessica and Steven for the moment. She wanted to ask Jessica where she and Todd had driven off to, but she just couldn't. *Maybe I'm afraid of the answer*, she thought. She felt tears starting to fill her eyes, but she willed herself not to cry. After all, she told herself, if Todd preferred Jessica—and that certainly was how it looked—she would not stand in the way. She'd do the decent thing. Die. Her unhappy thoughts were interrupted by Jessica's outraged cry.

"You didn't tell Steve about PBA? I simply don't understand how you could forget to tell him something so vital!"

"What about PBA?" Steven asked.

"We made it, Steve! We made it! Just today at lunch, Lizzie and I were accepted as full-fledged members of *the* most terrific sorority on campus!"

"No big deal," Elizabeth said.

"No big deal? Elizabeth, how can you say that?

How can you even think it? You've got to be seven hundred and thirty-seven kinds of idiots not to be excited about associating with the best girls at Sweet Valley High. What's wrong with you?"

"It's hard to get excited when your feet hurt," Elizabeth muttered.

"Your feet hurt? What in the world do your feet have to do with Pi Beta Alpha?" Jessica demanded.

"My feet always hurt when I have to walk all the way home from school," Elizabeth answered in an ominously quiet voice.

Sensing a crisis, Steven stood and said, "Hey, you two lovelies, I hate to eat and run, but I've got to go up and shower."

The twins ignored him. Their eyes were locked on one another.

"Look, I'll see you later," Steven said. "Take it easy on the guys this weekend. Broken hearts are not a lot of fun." He sighed, and there was a funny smile on his face.

Jessica turned suddenly toward Steven, grateful for an excuse to break away from Elizabeth's angry gaze. "Steve, I have the most terrific idea! If you're not busy this weekend, maybe you'd like me to arrange a date for you with Cara Walker," she said hopefully.

"Cara Walker?"

"You remember Cara, Steve—long dark hair,

terrific figure, fantastic tennis player. She's one of my best friends. She always thought you were soooo good-looking."

"Yeah, yeah, I remember. She's a cute kid, but a little young for me."

"Cara has become very mature, Steve. She's really ready to date a college man."

"Thanks, Jess, but no thanks. I have plans," he said, trying to edge out of the room.

"Plans? What kind of plans? Who is she?" Jessica shrieked.

" 'Who is she?' " Steven shrieked, mimicking Jessica.

"Well, you're coming home every weekend to see somebody," Jessica insisted. "Who is she? Somebody from college who lives in town?"

"Two nosy sisters are more than I need," Steven said, and there was an edge of anger in his voice. "See ya." He left the room quickly. They heard him go up the stairs and slam a door.

Jessica turned back to Elizabeth, who was brushing nonexistent crumbs from the butcher-block table.

"What's with him? Do you know who he's seeing?"

Elizabeth remained silent. She didn't trust herself to talk to her sister at this point.

Jessica fairly exploded. *What* is going on? Steve won't talk. You won't talk. The air in here

36

is so cold I can practically see my breath! I might as well be in Siberia!"

Wouldn't that be wonderful? Elizabeth thought.

"Lizzie, talk to me, please," Jessica coaxed. "You're mad at me, but I don't know why. Please, Lizzie." Her eyes sparkled with unshed tears.

Elizabeth turned to face Jessica, determined to have it out with her. But she weakened when she looked into her sister's face. Maybe nothing had happened with Jessica and Todd. Maybe it was all innocent, she thought. *And maybe I'm a world-class marshmallow!*

"Jess, I didn't really appreciate having to walk home today."

Quick as lightning, Jessica wailed, "You didn't! I saw you get into a car with a bunch of the kids and zoom off without me! You should have told me you were going to do that. What would have happened if Mom saw me driving the car? Do you want to get me into trouble? I think it was sneaky and rotten of you to leave me like that when it was your responsibility to bring me home in the car!"

"Jess, I didn't leave without you—I got held up in *The Oracle* and didn't get out until late."

"Oh. In that case, I forgive you. And I'm sorry I suspected you of trying to get me into trouble. I must have been mistaken about you getting into that other car. Now, let's talk about

Steve. He's up to something, and I think you know what it is."

"Whoa, Jess. Let's back up a bit. Jess? Jess!"

Jessica, her head in the refrigerator, didn't answer. Finally she turned, holding a plastic bag full of green grapes. "I was sure we had grapes! Now, about Steve."

"No, Jess," said a determined Elizabeth. "Let's talk about what happened after school. *I* saw *you* drive off in our car with Todd Wilkins." *Please let there be a reasonable explanation*, she prayed.

"Oh, that! I was just helping Todd." Jessica sat at the table popping grapes into her mouth while Elizabeth's world crumbled around her.

"Helping him?" Helping herself *to* him was more like it.

"He had to pick up some decorations for the dance, so I offered him a ride into town. He's so sweet, Liz."

I know, I know. Elizabeth moaned inwardly. "Jess, did he say anything about meeting some-one—or waiting for someone after school?"

Jessica rested her chin on one hand and thought for a moment. Putting her other hand behind her back, she crossed her fingers and finally answered, "I don't think so."

When it comes to being unforgettable, I have to be a minus ten, Elizabeth thought with disgust.

"Now can we talk about Steve?" Jessica said impatiently.

"What about him?"

"I don't believe you, Liz, I really don't. Our only brother is involved in a flaming love affair, and you don't care at all!"

"Steve? Flaming love affair?" Elizabeth shook her head in amazement. Was her sister trying to get off the subject of Todd, or did she know what she was talking about?

"It's totally obvious to anyone with half a brain that, *one*, Steve is involved with someone; *two*, that he hasn't said who it is; and *three*, that it must be someone we wouldn't like. And I'm going to find out what's going on!"

"Look, Sherlock," Elizabeth snapped, "has it ever occurred to you that, *one*, it's Steve's business; *two*, it's not our business; and *three*, you'd better butt out before Steve takes you apart?"

"You can do whatever you want, Elizabeth Wakefield, but it's just not in my nature to be cold and selfish when it comes to the happiness of a member of my family!" With an expression on her face that would make an angel envious, Jessica picked up her books and sailed out of the room.

In a rare display of temper, Elizabeth threw a sponge across the room, narrowly missing her mother, who stepped through the back door at that moment.

"Elizabeth, what in the world is going on here?"

"Oh! Mom. Nothing's going on. I was cleaning the table and the sponge just—just slipped out of my hand."

Alice Wakefield lowered the two grocery bags she was carrying onto the counter and gave her daughter a knowing look. "Something's wrong, honey, isn't it? Do you want to talk about it?" She walked over to Elizabeth and put her arm around her daughter's shoulder.

Elizabeth suddenly wished she were five years old again. Then she could cry and pour out all her troubles to her mother, who would make everything right. But that was then, and this was now.

Elizabeth shrugged off her mother's arm and walked over to pick up the sponge. "Mom, nothing is wrong!"

"Don't tell me nothing's wrong, Elizabeth. You're not acting like yourself at all. Now, talk to me, please. I have to meet a client, and I don't want to be late."

Count to ten, Elizabeth told herself. *Don't take your anger out on Mom.*

"Elizabeth, I'm waiting!"

And then she couldn't hold back her tears any longer. "Acting like myself—what's that,

Mom? Liz Wakefield is supposed to be good, sweet, kind, generous. . . ." The tears were streaming down her face. "Do you know what that adds up to, Mom? Boring, boring, boring! Sometimes I get hurt—sometimes I get angry. . . ."

"Honey, it's all right, I understand."

"Hey, is everybody in this family totally wacko?"

"Steve! I didn't know you were home."

"Hi, Mom. Bye, Mom." He dropped a kiss somewhere in the vicinity of his mother's forehead on his way to the door.

"Steve, I haven't had a chance to talk to you. Where are you going?"

"Out, Mom."

"Out? Out where? With whom?"

"Jeez! Is privacy a dirty word around here? The district attorney upstairs drove me up the wall with those kinds of questions. Fortunately, I was saved by the bell. The telephone bell. Sweet Jess is on the phone gushing all over some poor jerk named Todd. *Ciao*, you two!" Steven was out the door before Elizabeth or her mother could say another word.

Todd was on the phone with Jessica!

Elizabeth couldn't stand it one more minute. With tears streaming down her face, she threw the sponge in the sink and charged up to her room, leaving her mother openmouthed with surprise.

41

Four

Elizabeth's problems buzzed in her head like bees. Sitting in the *Oracle* office, she didn't know what to do first. She hadn't written a word for her "Eyes and Ears" column yet, and she still hadn't thought of a topic for her history paper. And then there was Steven—something was going on with him that wasn't quite right. It made her uneasy. And she couldn't get over an even more alarming suspicion about her father and Ms. West. She had seen Marianna recently, driving by with her father. She was a very beautiful woman. And she and her father had been so wrapped up in each other they hadn't even noticed Elizabeth. Even though she wanted to ignore it, Elizabeth smelled smoke. Did that mean there was fire?

She sighed. She didn't seem to have any answers lately. She looked down at her writing pad, which was absolutely blank except for the name Todd Wilkins scribbled across the top in large, dark letters. She knew it was hopeless to try to work when all she really wanted to do was lose herself in her special daydream. It was always the same funny little dream, but it made her feel so warm and good: They were sitting together, she and Todd, in the lunchroom at noon. It was jammed, and she was chattering on with Enid or some other friend when she became aware of Todd's hand affectionately caressing her hair. She turned to smile at him, and he pulled her close and kissed her gently on the forehead. That was it. Nothing more, but it was done right out there where everybody could see, as if it were the most natural thing in the world, Todd loving her. . . .

The daydream was like a favorite film Elizabeth played over and over again and never got tired of watching. That's what she was doing when Cara Walker burst noisily into the *Oracle* office, shattering the dream and bringing her back to her terrible reality.

"Liz," Cara gushed breathlessly, "I've got a great idea for an item."

"Good, Cara, what is it?"

"Well—do you know who writes the 'Eyes and Ears' column?"

"That's a secret, Cara. Nobody knows that except Mr. Collins."

"OK. Well, would you pass it on to him? The hottest new couple in the whole school is your very own sister Jessica—"

"Jessica?" Elizabeth asked, surprised.

"Yes! Now, I'm not a columnist," Cara gushed, "but the item could say something like—'The hottest new couple at Sweet Valley High is the co-captain of the cheerleaders and the captain of the basketball team!' "

"What?"

"See—they're both captains." Cara giggled. "That's why it's so neat!"

"Who told you about them?" Elizabeth asked, her heart thumping.

"It's all over school, Liz! Everybody's talking about it. They were driving around the other day in your mom's red convertible!"

"Oh."

"They were even seen up at Miller's Point," Cara continued. "And you know what goes on up there. Isn't it too much?" She sighed.

Elizabeth didn't even remember Cara running out. She felt totally destroyed. Todd and Jessica! Why did it have to be Jessica?

"Well, why not?" she heard herself saying aloud.

It was perfectly natural that Todd would like a terrific girl like her sister. Why shouldn't he?

44

Jessica was about the prettiest, most popular girl at Sweet Valley High.

And then a new, sinking realization shot through her heart like an arrow. Todd must have thought he was smiling at Jessica in the cafeteria the other day! She had built a fantasy, out of her own desires, about his feelings.

Well, at least that was clear now. Todd was interested in Jessica. Jessica knew it. And, as Cara had just said, the whole school knew it. Now at least she was sure what to write for the "Eyes and Ears" column. Elizabeth began typing it out, hardly noticing the tears that fell onto her typewriter keys.

No, she told herself sternly. *I won't be like this. I won't think about him anymore. Todd likes Jessica, and Jessica likes Todd, and that's that.*

She looked at what she had written:

"A certain tall, good-looking basketball player will be scoring high points off the court when he escorts a certain blond beauty who is co-captain of the cheerleading squad to the upcoming Phi Epsilon–Pi Beta Alpha dance."

Yes, Elizabeth told herself, *they're perfect for each other. I wish them the very best. I really do*, she insisted as she folded her head in her arms and sobbed.

"Elizabeth! What is it?"

She hadn't heard Mr. Collins walk in, yet

there he was, looking at her with concern, while tears slid down her face.

As usual, he knew what to do. Without another word he held out a crisp white handkerchief.

Elizabeth dabbed at her face, pulling herself together. She smiled weakly at the *Oracle*'s good-looking adviser, and thanked him for his handkerchief. "If you don't need it back right away, I'll launder it for you tonight," she offered.

Mr. Collins smiled. "I think I can manage without it," he answered. Then he asked gently, "Need to talk?"

She did need to talk to someone, and there weren't many people she trusted and respected more than Mr. Collins. She told him about her feelings for Todd and how he seemed to be interested in Jessica. "I'm so down."

"I know how you must feel." Roger Collins sighed sympathetically, pushing back a stray lock of his strawberry-blond hair. "But I've always found hard work to be the best painkiller. Come on, let us see your column. It'll take your mind off other things."

Elizabeth handed him her "Eyes and Ears" column.

"OK, here's this week's scoop," she said. But before Mr. Collins had a chance to look at it, John Pfeifer, the sports editor of *The Oracle*, came in all worked up.

"Hey, Mr. Collins," he said, "I'm the biggest idiot in the world. I've got the sports pages all laid out, and I can't find the picture of Todd Wilkins."

At the mention of his name, Elizabeth grabbed her things and dashed from the office. She didn't run far enough, though, because all of a sudden there he was in the flesh in the corridor. And with Jessica!

"No, really, Todd," Jessica was saying, "don't laugh. It's not funny. Really. I really am one of the most unpopular girls in school. Everyone else has a date for the dance. Really, everyone. Every single girl I know. Everyone but me."

Elizabeth made an about-face and walked quickly the other way.

But Todd had seen her. "Hey, Liz. What's your rush?"

She didn't answer. She kept moving. She had to get away.

"My sister." Jessica sighed and took Todd's arm. "Always in a hurry. Always rushing off to meet some guy."

"Where's she off to today?" asked Todd. "I was going up to the *Oracle* office to apologize in person. Hey, Jess, you explained about the other day, didn't you?"

"Oh, Todd, Liz is always ten steps ahead of me. I never know if she hears a word I'm saying.

I wonder who the lucky guy is today—probably her date for the frat dance."

"For the what?" said Todd.

"The frat dance—you know, the one your fraternity is holding with my sorority. Are you going?"

"Gee, I don't know," Todd said. "Are you?"

"That's what I was telling you. Don't you remember? You thought it was so funny that Jessica Wakefield is really a poor, lonely, miserable thing."

"Yeah, now I remember," Todd said. "But—are you sure Liz has a date for the dance?"

If it had been anyone else, Jessica would have blown up by now. But Todd Wilkins was so cute. She controlled herself and tried again.

"Todd, I told you. I can't keep up with her, so—it looks like you and I are in the same boat. The only ones."

"Hmm," Todd said, really getting her message for the first time. "So, you don't have a date, and I don't have a date. . . ."

"Yes? And?" Jessica smiled coaxingly.

But suddenly Todd looked over his shoulder as though he were searching for someone down the hall. "Uh, Jess, listen, don't worry about the dance. I'm sure a million guys are dying to ask you. Don't get uptight about it. I'm not. There's still plenty of time. Anyway, I've got to go. See you around."

Todd was gone before Jessica could recover. *I don't believe that guy!* she screamed to herself. If she had been home, she probably would have kicked a pillow across the room, maybe even cursed a little. But here in school she couldn't exactly make a scene.

Jessica felt a tiny twinge of panic. Why was Todd ignoring her? Had something happened to the Wakefield magic? *Impossible!* she told herself. She was still the most fantastic girl in school.

So why didn't Todd know it? Tears of angry frustration filled her eyes. She decided she would walk home from school. Whenever she was out walking, she never failed to attract a good deal of attention from passing cars.

The more the better, she thought, swinging her hips a little as she set off.

Five

"Pardon me, Heaven—which way to Mars?"

"What?" Jessica stared in astonishment at the boy leaning out the open window of the jacked-up Camaro.

She recognized him as Rick Andover, the most outrageous guy at Sweet Valley High—until he dropped out six months ago. Jessica found it hard to believe he was only seventeen. He looked older than most guys their age. He had the ice-cool handsomeness of a junior Clint Eastwood, and a hint of danger lurked in his sultry dark eyes. One elbow was hooked casually over the door. Jessica stared in fascination at the eagle emblem tattooed against the densely packed muscles of his forearm. Her stomach executed a slow somersault. She'd never been this close to Rick before.

"What are you staring at?" she finally asked, unnerved by the way his arrogant gaze raked over her.

One corner of his mouth turned up in a slow, sexy smile. "You," he answered. "I'm driving you home. That is, unless your mommy warned you never to take rides with strangers."

Jessica's eyes narrowed. Mr. Big-Shot Andover didn't know who he was talking to.

"I do as I please," she said, hesitating only a split second before she jumped into his car.

"I'm in for a lot of trouble." Rick grinned at her as they squealed away from the curb, shooting ahead of an elderly Pontiac, which had to slam on its brakes to keep from running into them.

"Why is that?" Jessica asked, a thrill that was half fear, half excitement racing up her backbone.

She'd heard a number of stories about Rick and the fast-lane life he led. He ran around with an older crowd and always had a lot of money in his pocket, even though it didn't look as if he had a job. He spent most of his time either working on his Camaro or cruising around in it—usually with a gorgeous girl at his side. Jessica squirmed with pleasure at having been selected as Rick's companion for that afternoon.

"Because *my* mother told *me* never to ride with strange young girls, that's why," said Rick.

"How do I know you won't try to take advantage of my innocence?"

Jessica giggled. She found Rick's sense of humor wickedly fascinating—like everything else about him.

"Don't worry," she replied, arching an eyebrow. "I'm fighting off the urge to attack you."

He shot her a look full of unmistakable meaning. "Just as long as you don't fight *too* hard. I'm not used to taking no for an answer."

Neither was Jessica, for that matter. At that moment she was reminded of Todd's indifference, which triggered a spurt of angry rebellion in her. She didn't resist as Rick's arm snaked around the back of the seat, his fingers squeezing her shoulder. She wished Todd could see her now. Maybe he would even be jealous.

"I'll pick you up at eight," Rick told her as they were cruising down Calico Drive, doing fifty in a thirty-five zone.

"What?"

He grinned. "Tomorrow, at eight. We've got a date, Heaven."

"But you never even *asked* me," she complained.

"I told you—I'm used to getting, not asking. Are you saying no?" he challenged, as if the thought were unheard of.

"No." She frowned slightly, biting her lip. "It's just that I'm not sure my parents—"

"Mommy and Daddy wouldn't like the idea of their Little Red Riding Hood going out with the Big Bad Wolf?" he supplied, sneering. "What do *you* want?"

He was looking at her in a way that made her skin tingle. His heavy-lidded eyes held a hypnotic hint of the excitement to come if she decided to go out with him. Jessica found it irresistible.

"Did you say eight?"

"Yeah." He gave her shoulder a harder squeeze. "Don't be late. We've got some serious boogeying to do. And, hey, forget about the folks, they don't even have to know you're out with me."

"Where should I meet you?" she asked.

"Right here," he answered, jerking to a noisy stop just around the corner from her house. "This is where you live, isn't it?"

She stared at him. "H-how did you know?"

"You're Jessica Wakefield, right? I make it a habit to know where all the foxiest chicks in Sweet Valley live."

Jessica felt herself grow warm all over. It was good to know she wasn't invisible to *every* boy in town! Maybe Rick wasn't Todd, but he wasn't exactly a clown like Winston Egbert, either. In fact, Rick Andover might just turn out to be fun. . . .

Before she could get out of the car, Rick pulled her close, giving her a light, teasing kiss on the mouth that promised more than it delivered. He smelled sexy, but in a strange way—like leather and gasoline.

"Where are we going tomorrow?" she asked as she was climbing out.

He winked suggestively. "That's for me to know and you to find out." He gunned the engine, drowning any protests she might have had. "Catch you later, Heaven."

The Camaro shot away from the curb, swerved in front of a bus, and ducked back into traffic just in time to miss a red Fiat coming up Calico Drive. Jessica shuddered. It was her mother!

The Fiat pulled over, and Alice Wakefield waved at Jessica.

"Jessica, hi! Come on, I'll give you a lift."

Jessica climbed in, her pulse still racing from her encounter with Rick.

"Did you see the boy driving that silver Camaro?" her mother fumed. "He almost ran into me!"

"Uh, no, I didn't see," Jessica stammered.

"It was that wild Rick Andover, I'm sure of it," she said.

Jessica bit her lip and said nothing.

"That kid is headed straight for trouble!" Mrs.

Wakefield pronounced with unusual vehemence, her expression darkening.

Jessica was surprised to see her mother so uptight. She was usually pretty calm about things! Come to think of it, she'd been uncharacteristically tense for the past week or so. Could it have something to do with the fact that both she and Dad had been working so hard lately—and spending so little time with each other? But Dad had Marianna West to keep him company during those late nights at the office. Marianna West was beautiful, divorced, and, most of all, available.

Jessica's thoughts whirled in panicked confusion. Poor Mom! Did she suspect as well?

"You look pretty dressed up for someone who's just going over to the library to do some studying," remarked Elizabeth as she observed her sister's elaborate preparations in front of the mirror. Come to think of it, Jessica *had* seemed strangely secretive throughout dinner, Elizabeth thought, as if she had something up her sleeve.

Jessica finished applying her lipstick, then stood back to examine herself in the mirror. Finally she turned to Elizabeth and gave her a sly smile, her aquamarine eyes sparkling with mischief.

"The truth is, I'm *not* going to the library," she confessed in a low voice. "But if you tell Mom, I'll boil you in oil."

"Where *are* you going, Jess?"

"I have a date." Jessica went back to admiring her reflection. "Do you think the red blouse would look better with this skirt, or my new yellow T-shirt?"

"Jess, stop changing the subject!" Elizabeth practically screamed at her. "Who are you going out with?"

Borrowing Rick's phrase, she answered coyly, "That's for me to know and you to find out."

Elizabeth frowned. She had a sick suspicion who Jessica was going out with, but it didn't make sense. Why should she have to sneak to go out on a date with Todd? Knowing her sister, it was just one of the many detours Jessica took off the straight and narrow in order to spice up her life. She stared at Jessica, who was bubbling over with excitement, and her heart sank.

She was certain Jessica was going out with Todd.

Six

"You're late," Rick said, gunning the engine impatiently as Jessica climbed in beside him. His dark eyes flickered over her. "But I can see it was worth the wait."

Jessica was glad she'd taken the trouble to curl her hair and put on her sexiest red blouse. She had even borrowed her sister's brand-new black sandal heels to go with her black silk-jersey skirt. She felt very grown-up, wedged beside Rick, with his arm clamped about her shoulders.

"Sorry, Rick," she breathed. "I had trouble getting away."

"Forget it. The night is young, and we've just begun, Heaven."

He pressed her even closer, turning his face briefly to nuzzle her hair. She caught the faint smell of cigarettes and liquor on his breath.

"Where are we going?" Jessica asked as Rick's Camaro shot over the winding valley road leading to the coast highway. Before he could say anything, she answered her own question: "I know—that's for you to know and me to find out, right?"

"Right. Hey, you're a fast learner. I can't wait to see what else you're good at."

Jessica shivered a little at his compliment. He talked the way he drove—fast and dangerously. For an instant she wondered if she would be able to keep him at bay, but she quickly dismissed the worry. She had yet to come up against a situation she couldn't handle.

Even so, nothing could squelch the nervous fluttering in her stomach as Rick's car spun to a stop in a shower of gravel in front of a seedy-looking beachfront roadhouse. A red, blinking neon sign advertised that it was Kelly's. Loud music spilled from the open doorway, punctuated by harsh bursts of laughter.

None of Jessica's friends had ever been inside Kelly's. It had the most notorious reputation of any bar in the whole valley. A mixture of alarm and excitement raced through Jessica's body. Boy, would she have something to talk about tomorrow!

Rick must have noticed how nervous she

looked, for he squeezed her shoulders in rough reassurance. "Take it easy, Heaven. You've just graduated into the real world. Think you can handle it?"

"Are you kidding?" she tossed back. "I can handle anything."

Once inside, she wasn't so sure. Kelly's was definitely out of her league. So was Rick Andover, she was beginning to think.

"That's my girl," he murmured against her ear, sliding his arm about her waist in a proprietary way as they passed through the bar area, heading for one of the dimly lit booths in back.

Jessica had never been so acutely aware of both her age and her appearance before. Several of the men stared at her, and one let forth a low wolf whistle. Her face was burning from anger and embarrassment, and her eyes watered from the cigarette smoke that wreathed the cramped room. As they slid into the cracked vinyl booth, she leaned over to tell Rick how uncomfortable she felt, but her words were drowned in a sudden burst of twangy country-western music from the jukebox.

Rick ordered a couple of boilermakers, something Jessica had never heard of before. She was relieved to see that it was only beer, until the waitress placed two shot glasses of whiskey beside their foaming mugs. She didn't even look at Jessica, much less ask for her I.D., despite the sign hanging over the bar: MINORS WILL NOT BE SERVED UNDER PENALTY OF LAW. With a growing sense of unease, Jessica sipped her beer while Rick tipped back his glass of whiskey as though it were water.

He laughed huskily. "Not exactly prom time, huh?" His hand found her knee under the table and gave it a squeeze.

Jessica winced but forced a smile anyway. "It's . . . it's fun," she agreed, lying through her gritted teeth.

"So are you." Rick's hand moved up an inch or two on her leg. "I knew the minute I laid eyes on you that you wouldn't let me down, little Jessica."

Jessica shifted her position, trying to maneuver herself out of his reach, but Rick only squeezed tighter. She giggled nervously in an attempt to cover up her unease.

"And I should have known you were the kind of guy who couldn't keep his hands to himself," she scolded lightly.

Rick's eyes narrowed. "All tease and no tickle, huh? Didn't your mommy tell you not to put anything in the window that you don't sell in the store?" His fingers groped higher, and she noticed he was beginning to slur his words. "Well, I've seen the merchandise, baby, and I'm sold."

This time there was no pretense in the way

Jessica pulled away from Rick. Suddenly he didn't seem so fascinating anymore. Just dangerous. His eyes looked flat and black, like a snake's. His breath, as he leaned over to kiss her, reeked of alcohol.

"Rick, don't—" Jessica turned her head so that his lips found only her cheek, leaving a wet imprint, like the rings of moisture left on the table by their glasses.

"Whatsa matter?" he drawled. "You wanna go somewhere quieter? Listen, I know a place down the—"

"No!" Jessica cried in true alarm. "Rick, take me home. I—I told my parents I'd be back in an hour. I really can't stay."

He shrugged. "So call and tell 'em you'll be late. 'Less you're afraid of turning into a pumpkin." Rick laughed loudly at his own joke.

"Rick, *please*." She wasn't in the habit of begging, but she was getting desperate. A few more drinks and Rick would be in no condition to drive her home. Then she'd really be stuck.

"Forget it, baby." He gulped the last of his beer and finished off her untouched shot of whiskey. "I came here for a good time, and I'm not leaving."

"What about *me*?" she wailed, suddenly close to tears. "What am *I* supposed to do?"

Rick hooked a tattooed arm around her neck, dragging her into another one of his moist kisses.

"Do I have to spell it out for you? Relax, baby. You might even have a good time yourself."

Jessica slithered adroitly from his drunken clinch and stood up. "Sorry, Rick," she said, in command of herself once again, "but I'd have a better time with an octopus. Thanks for nothing. I think I'll just call a cab."

"Wait a minute," Rick hissed, grabbing her hand and jerking her back into the booth. "You're not going anywhere!"

Jessica let out a yelp as blunt fingers encircled her wrist. She struggled to free herself. A man sitting at a bar stool nearby swiveled around to see what was going on.

"He giving you trouble, miss?" the man asked.

"Yes," Jessica announced in a loud voice. "I have to go home, and he won't let me go!"

The man grinned. He was probably about her father's age, only rougher looking—in a funny kind of nice way. Like a cross between a teddy bear and *Jaws*.

"I'd be glad to give you a lift home if your boyfriend won't," he said.

"Thanks," Jessica said, "but he's not my boyfriend."

She had succeeded in wrenching away and was halfway to the door when Rick lunged after her, his black eyes spitting fire.

"Out of the way, lard bucket!" he growled at the man, who had stepped in front of him.

At that moment Jessica felt as if all the air in that smoky room had been sucked out. She could hardly breathe. As she watched in horror, Rick hunched forward, swinging his fist in a wide, drunken arc. The man easily blocked the punch. His own ham-sized fist exploded against Rick's jaw with an audible crack. Rick reeled backward, crashing into a table and knocking over several chairs. A trickle of blood oozed from one corner of his mouth.

Jessica stood frozen, unaware that any time had passed, until the howl of a siren brought her back to her senses with a sickening snap. The next thing she knew, there were two policemen barreling into the bar. One of them headed straight for Rick, who lay sprawled on the floor amid the cigarette butts, mumbling curses at everyone in sight.

"This time I'm pressing charges," the bartender was yelling. "His name's Andover, and this isn't the first time he's tried to bust up my place!"

The other policeman took Jessica aside. "Do your parents know you're here, young lady?" he demanded sternly.

"Oh, no, please, *please* don't tell them," she begged, tears pouring down her cheeks. She didn't have to turn on the waterworks—this time they were for real. "They would just *kill* me if they found out!"

"I doubt that," he answered, but his tone softened slightly. "Maybe it's best for your parents to find out. They might stop you from doing something even worse the next time. Now, why don't you give me your name?"

Panic swept through Jessica. Arrested! Taken home by the police from Kelly's! She'd be absolutely ruined—besides being grounded for five hundred years!

"Uh . . . Wakefield . . ." she managed to choke.

"Wakefield, huh?" The cop peered closely at her. "Sure, I know you. You're a friend of my niece, Emily Mayer. I've heard her mention Elizabeth Wakefield."

"Emily? Oh, sure!" Jessica ignored his mistake. "Emily's a terrific drummer, and the Droids are the hottest band in Sweet Valley," she babbled in relief.

The cop jotted something down in his notebook "OK, young lady," he said. "Let's get you home where you belong."

In the squad car Jessica began sobbing again with renewed desperation. She pulled out all the stops—every plea she could think of, from the trauma of being scarred for life to the fact that her father was a lawyer, and his reputation could be ruined. The cop said nothing until he'd pulled to a stop in front of her house.

Then he turned to her. "Listen," he said, giving her a long, hard look. "I'm going to let you off *this* time. No thanks to Niagara Falls, either. I just happen to believe in second chances."

"Oh, *thank* you, Officer!" Jessica leaped from the car like someone who had just been reprieved from death row. "I *swear* it'll never happen again!"

"It'd better not," he called after her as she bounded up the driveway. "Stay away from Rick Andover. I don't want to see you in the middle of any more brawls at Kelly's. And keep in mind, Elizabeth, I don't believe in third chances."

"Wait, I'm not—" She started to tell him she wasn't Elizabeth. Now that she was out of danger, she was suddenly stricken by a guilty conscience for letting him think she was her twin. But the squad car had already disappeared into the night.

Blinded by her overwhelming relief, Jessica hadn't seen the girl who walked past with a little black poodle on a leash. She probably wouldn't have noticed it was Caroline Pearce, her sorority sister and three-doors-down neighbor, even if she'd bumped into her. Jessica was so happy to have been let off the hook, she practically flew up the front steps to her house.

Caroline was heading home, too, straight for the white Princess phone in her bedroom, which served as the central switchboard for Sweet Valley High gossip. . . .

Seven

Elizabeth looked out her bedroom window to see what kind of day it was. No big surprise. The morning was bright and sunny, as it almost always was in Sweet Valley. *Why can't you get a cloudy day when you really need one?* she mused. *OK, Liz,* she told herself sternly. *Get your act together.* If Todd preferred Jessica, that's the way it was.

Elizabeth scanned the room. It was her haven, her sanctuary. She had decorated it herself. She had chosen the off-white carpeting, had painted the walls a soft cream, and had picked out the bed frame and matching dresser. She had also put up the two mirrors in the room, a small one over the dresser and a full-length one on the back of the door. One whole wall was a closet with louvered doors.

Instead of a desk, Elizabeth had decided on a large rectangular table. It held her typewriter, reference books, paper, and a ceramic holder for pens and pencils. And right above the table was a theater poster of Jason Robards in *A Touch of the Poet*. She didn't think she would ever be as good a writer as Eugene O'Neill, but it was a terrific-looking poster—and she *was*, after all, a writer.

Elizabeth looked longingly at the one curious piece of furniture in the room, a chaise longue she had found in a thrift shop and re-covered in a soft, pale velvet. Maybe she could just curl up there for the day, or maybe for the rest of her life. Then her eyes zeroed in on the digital clock-radio on her nightstand. *Oh, no,* she thought. *I'm not only miserable down to my toes, but I'm going to get an F in science if I miss Mr. Russo's test!*

She grabbed her knapsack and dashed out of the room, nearly knocking over Jessica, who was heading for the stairs.

"Liz!" Jessica yelped.

"Sorry, Jess. I just checked the time. We're going to be late! Are you ready for Russo's test?"

"Tests! Tests! Tests!" Jessica grumbled as the two went down the stairs. "Doesn't that man realize there are more important things to do at school besides take tests? Of course I'm not ready!"

Elizabeth headed for the front door. "I don't have time for breakfast. See you in school!"

"Wait, Liz, there's something I have to talk to you about. It's absolutely urgent!"

"No time, Jess. I promised Enid I'd meet her before first period. Later!" And she was gone before Jessica could tell her about the night before.

"Well, if meeting that wimpy Enid Rollins is more important than talking to her own sister . . ." Jessica muttered. Maybe nobody at school would find out about last night, she thought. "Yeah, fat chance. Maybe school will be canceled on account of a snowstorm."

Elizabeth spotted Enid sitting by herself. As she made her way across the broad green lawn, Elizabeth wondered what the latest "absolutely vital" matter was that Enid wanted to see her about. As she passed a group of boys, she noticed that they were staring at her. Before she could check to be sure she had all her clothes on, Bruce Patman stepped out of the group. He was smirking.

"Didn't know you had it in you, Wakefield. Really awesome."

"What?" Elizabeth stopped short and faced Bruce.

"You know, Wakefield, you know. And now I know."

"The only thing I know, *Patman*, is that you seem to be missing a few marbles," Elizabeth snapped. She turned her back on the group and walked over to Enid.

"Liz, I thought you'd never get here," Enid said, jumping to her feet.

"I just got waylaid by Mr. Wonderful," Elizabeth said, nodding in Bruce Patman's direction.

"You mean *the* gorgeous Bruce Patman?"

"Don't forget rich, Enid."

"Oh, yes. Gorgeous, rich, and let's not leave out—*ta da!*—star of the tennis team." Both girls started giggling. Most girls at Sweet Valley High would kill for a date with the son of the town's richest and oldest family, but not Elizabeth or Enid.

Suddenly getting serious, Enid asked, "What was Bruce saying to you?"

Elizabeth thought for a moment. "I'm not sure. He was totally weird. He said something about not knowing I had it in me, whatever *it* is."

"Oh." Enid looked down at her shoes.

"Oh? Do you know what he was talking about?"

"I'm not sure, but I think so. Liz, I want you

to know that you're my best friend. And I'll always be *your* best friend, no matter what."

"No matter what? Enid, what are you talking about?"

"I know something about making mistakes, Liz, and I meant it when I said we're friends. I don't want you to worry about losing my friendship. Ever."

Elizabeth stared openmouthed at her friend. What was the matter with everybody today?

"Enid, get to the point! Have I suddenly grown another head?"

"Liz, I know there are some things you think you can never tell anybody, but—oh, there's Ronnie waving at me. I have to talk to him before first bell." Enid seemed almost relieved to delay her conversation with her friend. "I'll talk to you later. Bye!"

Elizabeth stared in complete puzzlement as Enid hurried across the lawn toward Ronnie Edwards, who stood there frowning.

"Is something wrong, Ronnie?" Enid would die if Ronnie were mad at her. She felt her heart begin to race.

"Why were you talking to *her*?" he asked, still frowning.

"To Liz? She's my best friend!"

"Maybe you should be more careful about

choosing friends. Everybody's talking about that stunt she pulled last night."

"Everybody? Ronnie, that's not true. Besides, we haven't heard Liz's side yet."

"Enid, it's all over campus. Caroline Pearce saw the squad car bring Liz home. She went to Kelly's with Rick Andover and started a riot. You really want to be friends with someone like that?" Ronnie said accusingly.

"We're not sure about all that, Ronnie. It's just a lot of rumors. I can't believe she'd go out with Rick. She's my friend, and I'm going to stick by her, no matter what."

The sound of the bell cut off whatever Ronnie was going to say. But Enid knew he was angry.

What an absolutely unbelievable day, Elizabeth thought as she reached her front door. It was like being in the *Twilight Zone.* Everywhere she went, she got strange looks. Kids stopped talking as soon as she approached—in the lunchroom, in the library, in the halls. And what in the world was Enid trying to tell her?

Even Mr. Collins had insisted on being mysterious about some kind of problem with the school football field. She remembered her father mentioning the same thing the other morning at breakfast, but he wouldn't elaborate, either. It was spooky, and the day wasn't over yet.

As soon as she opened the door, Elizabeth heard angry voices coming from the kitchen.

"Steve, you were supposed to go back to school last night," Alice Wakefield said.

"Mom, don't get uptight. I didn't miss anything important today."

"That's not the point. You're being very secretive. Your father and I are concerned about you."

"I didn't know you and Dad had time for anything except work these days."

"Steve!"

"Sorry, Mom. I just don't like being hassled. Look, I've got to go. See you Friday."

Elizabeth entered the room just as Steven was opening the back door.

"Bye, Liz. Bye, Mom." He was gone.

Elizabeth and her mother exchanged confused looks.

"What's with Steve, Mom?"

"I was hoping you could tell me."

"I don't—"

The sharp ring of the phone interrupted Elizabeth.

"I'll get it, Mom! Hello?" She covered the mouthpiece with her hand. "It's for me. I'll take it on the upstairs extension. Hang it up for me, Mom."

"Sure. Then I've got to meet a client. Dad will be late, too. And there's a casserole in the freezer for you and Jessica," she said, having to shout the last because Elizabeth was already upstairs. She was her usual organized self, but she sounded distracted, as if she had her own problems as well.

"Enid!" Elizabeth nearly shouted into the phone. "Talk to me! Tell me what's going on!"

Less than a minute later, a stunned Elizabeth was gasping for breath.

"I don't believe this! *I* was arrested, put on parole, and brought home in a squad car! Enid, that is the wildest, most idiotic, most— In Kelly's with Rick Andover? No wonder everybody—! They're lies, Enid, I would never . . . !"

When Elizabeth stopped to catch her breath, Enid filled her in on all the gruesome details.

"Caroline Pearce said she saw you, Liz. She said the policeman called you by name, that he has your name in his book, and that you're on parole! But, Liz, you and I are friends, no matter—"

"Stop saying that, Enid! There is no 'matter.' I don't know why Caroline would spread lies about me. For heaven's sake, I've never even spoken to Rick Andover!"

In a flash, though, Elizabeth realized that she did know someone who would speak to him— Jessica! But Caroline had heard the policeman say Elizabeth, not Jessica. She had to get to the bottom of this. There was only one person who would have the answers, and that blond duplicate of herself should be home any minute.

"Enid, I don't know how in the world all this started, but I can't talk any more now," she said abruptly. "I'll call you back later. Bye!"

She hung up and went into her room. She paced from the window to the door, waiting for her sister to get home.

It was a nightmare. Please let it be a nightmare! But Elizabeth knew she was wide awake. Suddenly the most awful, totally terrible thought popped into her head. Todd! Todd Wilkins had heard this story! Maybe he even believed it! *I've got to tell him the truth*, she decided. But what *was* the truth?

The front door slammed, and a breathless Jessica ran upstairs, calling, "Liz! Liz, where are you?"

Jessica bolted into Elizabeth's room. The sisters stood facing one another, identical expressions on their lovely faces. Total panic.

"You've heard. I can tell you've heard, Lizzie!"

"Have I ever!"

"A thing like this could ruin the entire family, our futures!" She moaned. "What are we going to do?"

"Let's start with Rick Andover, Jess."

"Rick Andover? What's he got to do with anything?"

"He has everything to do with all the kids in

school thinking I have a police record and that I'm out on parole!" Elizabeth shouted, for once making no effort to control her temper.

"Oh, that." Jessica shrugged, flushing guiltily. "I can clear that little thing up in no time."

"Do it *now*!" Elizabeth said.

"*Later*, Liz! I'm talking about something *really* important. I found out this afternoon why Steve has been coming home every weekend. No wonder he's been so mysterious and obnoxious to everybody. He should be ashamed of himself! My whole life is going to go right down the tubes! How could he do this, Lizzie?" She began to cry.

"Stop babbling, Jess! And stop crying! Tell me what Steve has done."

"Our brother, a member of the Wakefield family, has been spending every weekend," Jessica got out between sobs, "with Betsy Martin!"

A stunned silence filled the room. Elizabeth plopped down onto her bed, all thoughts of her own troubles pushed aside. Steven was seeing Betsy Martin?

"Jess, are you sure? I can't believe it. Betsy's been doing drugs for years—she sleeps around—"

"And her father gets bombed out of his mind every night," Jessica said wildly.

A new worry occurred to Elizabeth. "Jess, what are Mom and Dad going to say when they find out?"

"Mom and Dad? Liz, what about the kids? I will be totally ruined forever when this gets around school! And you, too."

"*I'm* ruined already," Elizabeth cried. "Will you please tell me what this Rick Andover business is all about!"

"Later, Lizzie, please."

"No, I want to know *right now*!"

Eight

"Oh, Lizzie, it was so awful!" Jessica wailed, bursting into tears. "There was drinking and fighting, and Rick had his hands all over—"

"Rick!" Elizabeth cut in. "Did you say *Rick*? You mean you weren't with Todd?" Elizabeth was so relieved, she felt her anger deflate like a punctured balloon.

"I wish I *had* been with Todd," said Jessica. "He would never have taken me to that awful place! I'm telling you, it was all Rick's fault. He practically *dragged* me in there, for heaven's sake!"

"If it was all Rick's fault," Elizabeth asked, suspiciously, "then how come the police ended up with *my* name?" She wasn't letting Jessica worm her way out of it this time.

"It was a mix-up, Liz," Jessica cried. "You've

got to believe me! The cop was Emily's uncle, and he said he recognized you, and—"

"And you didn't correct him." Elizabeth's voice was hard.

"I tried to, Lizzie. Honest, I did. He—he wouldn't listen."

Jessica was sobbing uncontrollably now. Elizabeth felt torn between wanting to comfort her sister and wanting to murder her. Knowing she'd been with Rick instead of Todd made it easier for Elizabeth to forgive her.

"Stop crying, Jess," she commanded softly. "I know how scared you must have been. I guess I would've been, too. What I don't understand is how you could let people think *I* was arrested."

"That's so totally ridiculous," she said, grabbing a handful of tissues and mopping her face. "The cop just drove me home and gave me a warning. If I'd been arrested, Mom and Dad would've been called. I can't believe Caroline would spread a story like that about you!"

"I suppose this whole thing is Caroline's fault now, huh?"

"*Please* don't hate me," Jessica begged. "I'll clear your name, Liz. I promise. Even if it ruins me." She sneaked a look at her sister to see if she would demand such a sacrifice.

Elizabeth just thought for a moment.

"But you know, Liz, doing that just might
79

keep the gossip going on *forever*. You know how it is. Anyway, something will happen tomorrow, and everybody will forget about this," she said hopefully.

"Jessica, I don't care about the whole world. I just want my friends to know the truth."

Jessica sensed she was almost off the hook.

"Certainly you don't think your friends—your *real* friends—would think you were arrested. Don't tell me that your *very best* friend, wimpy Rollins, would turn on you?"

Jessica knew she shouldn't make a crack about Enid, but she couldn't resist. She didn't like Elizabeth being close friends with anyone but her.

Lost in thought, Elizabeth mumbled, "No, Enid is my friend. She'll stick." *But what about Todd?* she thought.

"Is there anyone else you want me to tell the truth to? Maybe Todd Wilkins? Are you and he kind of *buddies*?" Jessica asked, never taking her eyes off her sister's face.

Buddies? Buddies! The one boy in all the world whom Elizabeth loved, who made her heart beat faster and her breath catch in her throat. Buddies?

"Yeah, I guess that's what we are," she finally answered.

Knowing she had won the battle, Jessica gave Elizabeth a hug. "Don't worry about a thing,

Liz. Todd and I have gotten very close. I'll tell him the truth. I just know he's too terrific a guy to hold it against you. No way do I want him mad at you, Lizzie. Like, wouldn't it be impossible when he picks me up for dates for him not to say hello to you, at least?"

The picture of a smiling Todd picking up Jessica for dates, holding her hand—kissing her good night at the front door—made Elizabeth want to weep. She could only imagine in despair what Todd must think of her now. . . .

Ronnie and Enid had a date to spend what was left of the day at the beach, but when Ronnie knocked on Enid's door, Todd was standing beside him.

"You don't mind, do you, Enid?" Ronnie asked as they clattered down the deck steps. "Just look at Todd. He's a mess. I couldn't let a frat brother go moping around like that without doing something. So I asked him to come along with us today, OK?"

Enid took one look at Todd's sheepish, embarrassed expression and melted. She ruffled his hair, linked arms with the both of them, and said, "Come on, you gorgeous guys. Let's go!"

At first the job of cheering Todd up didn't appear to be very difficult. By the time they hit the blue-green water, he was actually laughing.

Immediately Enid and Ronnie announced, "It's water war time!" and splashed Todd from both sides. They all rode in on the waves like human surfboards. When they finally dragged themselves from the water, dripping and shivering, they were all in great spirits. That is, until Ronnie, sitting cross-legged on the small blanket Enid had brought along, said, "Hey, what do you think of Liz Wakefield and Rick Andover?"

Todd sat upright, scowling. "I heard the rumor," he muttered unhappily. He looked crushed.

Enid glared at Ronnie for being so stupid, but he didn't seem to get the message.

"That guy is such a beast. I can't believe her!" Ronnie added, not realizing he was rubbing salt in the wound.

"Now, wait a minute," Enid said. "We've all heard the same rumor and—"

"See?" Ronnie interrupted. "Even Liz's best friend—"

"No, no!" Enid protested. "We've just heard the rumor. But I know it's not true. I asked her about it."

Smiling sarcastically, Ronnie demanded, "And what did poor Liz do? Burst into tears?"

Enid didn't like Ronnie's attitude. "No, she didn't burst into tears. In fact, she seemed quite angry and confused that anybody would say such things about her. She flatly denied the rumor, Ronnie."

"And you believed her?" Ronnie asked, amazed.

"Of course I believed her!" Enid said hotly. "She wouldn't lie to me. She's my best friend!"

Sitting on the plaid blanket in the blazing sun, the three friends shared an awkward silence. Enid picked up handfuls of sand, letting the grains sift out from between her clenched fingers. "I know Liz better than just about anybody. And I can't imagine her with a guy like Rick— especially in a place like Kelly's."

"Well, sometimes a person is not what she *seems*," Ronnie said sharply.

Todd nodded in agreement. "Yeah, that's true. I mean, that's what I'm finding."

Enid couldn't believe her ears and told them so. "I know there's another explanation. I can't accept these rumors, especially after Liz has denied them."

Todd, a sad, faraway look in his brown eyes, said, "Maybe there's just so much a person can take. I mean, how long can you go on trusting someone, believing in someone?"

"If you're her friend," Enid said, "you should never stop."

Todd looked down at the sand.

Desperately, Enid turned to Ronnie. "Sometimes people make mistakes they're sorry for later," she said slowly and from her heart. "Don't you think they should be forgiven?"

Ronnie thought for a moment, throwing a pebble over and over into the sand. Finally he shook his head. "Some things are unforgivable."

Enid was shaken by Ronnie's attitude. It was a side of him she hadn't known before—a cold, hard, unforgiving side—and it frightened her.

"How did you hear about Liz?" Todd asked Ronnie.

"I heard it from at least three people," Ronnie answered. "She was seen getting out of the police car. She was overheard promising never to go to Kelly's again—with Rick, especially."

"Well, I guess that's it, then," Todd said with bitter resignation. "There's no use arguing because it's a plain fact—Liz was there with Rick, and no amount of explaining can change that."

"Well, I don't believe she was there," Enid said, "but even if she was, the real question is, are you a true friend, and can you forgive her?" She was really asking Ronnie, pleading with Ronnie, but it was Todd who answered.

"I don't know. I really don't."

"Well, I *do* know," Ronnie said vehemently. "And if a girl I liked did something like that, I'd never speak to her again."

Though the day was still warm, Enid shivered and pulled on a shirt. She had made a decision. *He must never know about me. Never.* He must never know about the time she was arrested after that horrible accident. Lost in thought about herself, Enid forgot all about Elizabeth's problems.

Nine

It was one of those mornings that made Elizabeth think her sister had been a bird in a former life. Jessica was chirping away nonstop at the breakfast table.

"Didn't I tell you, Miss Sourpuss, that it would all blow over?" Jessica burbled over her Rice Krispies. "Why, the entire school has totally forgotten about you and Rick."

"About who and who?"

"I mean about Rick and me. Nobody has said a word to me about it in days."

"How nice for you, Jess. They've talked to me about it. Practically *all* anybody talks about is me going to Kelly's and what I did with Rick."

"Who said that?"

"Actually, Jessica, you're right. Nobody talks

about it. They just *hint*! They talk to each other about it, but when I walk up, they stop. I'm a walking conversation stopper."

"I think you're just imagining things."

"No I'm not, Jessica. Enid filled me in. Everybody's talking about me and Rick, and they all believe it. On Wednesday there was a big message on the blackboard in the *Oracle* office when I walked in, too."

Jessica leaned forward. "What did it say?" she asked, as though it were some juicy gossip about somebody else.

"It said: 'Scoop! Big-shot editor Wakefield makes news! Why isn't it in the paper?' "

"That is vile," Jessica snapped. *"You're* not the editor! It isn't your decision to print such a story."

Elizabeth shook her head in dismay. "Jessica, sometimes I truly do wonder about you."

"Lizzie, I *promise* that anytime I hear anybody say anything about you, I'll set them straight."

Elizabeth stared forlornly out the window at the peaceful swimming pool. Wouldn't it be nice to sit out there all day and not have to face anyone at Sweet Valley High?

"Are there people you're worried about?" Jessica asked anxiously. "Because I'll tell them, if there are."

If only someone could convince Todd Wilkins

of the truth. Elizabeth felt tears forming behind her eyes. Enid had told her about their trip to the beach and how Todd had heard all the lurid details and believed them. How could he?

"No," said Elizabeth. "Anybody who would believe things about me without even finding out the truth isn't anybody I care about."

"You're not going to tell Mom and Dad on me?"

"Jessica, you know I'd never do something like that to you."

Jessica gazed at her wonderful sister, and a wave of love flooded through her. She grabbed Elizabeth and hugged her.

"You're so wonderful to me, Lizzie! Sometimes I think I don't deserve it!"

In Elizabeth's mood, that was all it took for the tears to flow. She wept, hugging Jessica as hard as she could. "Oh, Jessie, you're wonderful, too. You deserve everything. Everybody loves you, and they should."

"Lizzie—you're crying!"

"It's all right, Jessie. I'm just upset—about Steve and—things." And she hurried from the kitchen to fix her face. She would show none of this at school. Elizabeth Wakefield would hold her head high.

Actually, the gossip about the Kelly's Roadhouse fiasco did seem to be dying down. When Elizabeth got to school that day, the corridors were buzzing with a new and much more serious crisis—the Gladiators' football field. George Fowler—Lila Fowler's father—was throwing the school off the field, the rumor said. He was one of the richest men in Sweet Valley already, and he wanted to take over the football field to put up a factory. Now the big mystery of the football field made sense.

"George Fowler is stealing our football field," lanky, dark-haired Winston Egbert told Elizabeth breathlessly. For once, he didn't appear to be joking.

"No, you idiot," said Dana Larson, who was walking by. Dana was the lead singer for the Droids, Sweet Valley High's hottest rock band. "It's the Patmans. Bruce Patman's father has bought the land, and he's going to put in an amusement park."

"An amusement park?" said Winston, astounded. "Hey, that wouldn't be so bad!" He turned and dashed down the corridor. "Hey, did you hear? Bruce Patman's father is building a Disneyland on the football field."

Elizabeth, from her experience as a reporter for *The Oracle*, knew there was no sense believing the distorted rumors circulating through the halls. She headed for the newspaper office and Mr. Collins.

"Mr. Collins," she said, "what's going on? I've heard crazy rumors."

"They're not rumors, Elizabeth," said Mr. Collins, looking grim. "They're true enough."

Sweet Valley's two most powerful families, the Patmans and the Fowlers, were at each other's throats again, and the high school was caught in the middle. The Patman-Fowler feud—pitting the old, established Henry Wilson Patman and his canning industry money against George Fowler and his new money made through silicon chips—was going to be fought out on the Gladiators' football field.

"The school had leased the field from the city, but the lease ran out recently," said Mr. Collins. "Now George Fowler is trying to buy the land so he can put up a new factory."

"Right across from the school?" said Elizabeth, aghast.

"That's what he wants. The Fowlers judge everything by how they can make more money."

"But where would the Gladiators play football?"

"I don't think that interests George Fowler, Liz."

"But I heard the Patmans want the field, Mr. Collins."

"Oh, yes, they do. When they heard George Fowler was going to buy the land for a factory, they went into shock. They've gotten a court injunction to block the sale. They don't want a factory there."

"Well, good," said Elizabeth. "Then we support the Patmans."

"Wrong, Elizabeth. The Patmans don't want the Gladiators on the field either. They want to plant a formal English garden, the way it was in 1916 when it was part of the Vanderhorn estate."

"Who were the Vanderhorns?"

"The Vanderhorns were one of the original families in Sweet Valley."

"So?"

"Bruce Patman's mother was a Vanderhorn."

"My goodness," said Elizabeth. "What a mess."

"Yes. And I'm afraid it's all yours."

"Mine?" Elizabeth felt her pulse racing. She had never been given a story this big before.

"Yes. John is busy with the game against Palisades High. If we ever get to play it. So this one's all yours."

"You mean we might not be able to use the field for the Palisades game, Mr. Collins?"

"As of right now, Elizabeth, nobody can use the field for anything. The Fowlers have claimed it, and the Patmans' court injunction keeps everybody off the land until this is settled."

"But the team has to practice!"

"Not on their own field, Elizabeth. Have fun."

Court injunctions might keep school officials and even big shots like the Patmans and the

Fowlers off a disputed football field, but they were useless against the student body of Sweet Valley High. By lunchtime the rumors had totally engulfed the school. Kids were milling around in front on the steps and spilling over onto the lawn.

In the middle of the throng was Ken Matthews, the powerful blond captain of the Gladiators' football team. Next to him was Todd Wilkins and some of the other school jocks. All eyes were turned to them. Something had to be done.

"What are we going to do, Kenny?" somebody yelled. "They can't take our field."

"OK, calm down," Ken said, gazing out over the crowd. "Don't worry. Number one, the Gladiators have never lost anything without a fight!"

A roar of approval greeted this comment.

"And, number two," Todd added, "we need that field more than anyone else. They can build a factory or a garden anyplace!"

"Right on," somebody yelled.

"And it's ours!" Ken shouted.

Another roar from the assembled students.

Looking out the cafeteria window, Mrs. Waller, the school dietitian, saw the rally building in size. She put down her clipboard and hurried down the corridor to the gym.

"Coach!" Mrs. Waller called out.

Coach Schultz looked up from the play diagrams he was working on in preparation for the big game against the Palisades Pumas.

"What's the matter, Mrs. Waller?"

"Coach, I think we've got trouble. The football team is out in front of the school, and they're all worked up."

"My team?" said Coach Schultz, getting up quickly.

"Kenny Matthews is in the middle of it."

"What are we waiting for?"

And together, Coach Schultz and Mrs. Waller hurried upstairs toward the principal's office.

"Chrome Dome's going to have a fit," said Mrs. Waller.

"My boys won't do anything wrong," said Coach Schultz. "They're just high-spirited."

They swept into Mr. Cooper's office in time to hear the announcement on the school's intercom system.

"Coach Schultz, please report to the principal's office!"

"What are we going to do?" Jessica shouted, having pushed through the crowd to head up the cheerleaders.

"I'll tell you what we're going to do," Todd yelled. "We're going to stage a sit-in right on the football field!"

93

A cheer went up.

"If they want to build anything on this field, they're going to have to build it on top of us," Ken shouted to the crowd.

Another cheer went up, and the students began rushing across the great lawn toward the field.

"Come on!" Jessica yelled, piloting the cheerleaders.

"Follow me, Gladiators," Ken shouted.

And just like an army of Roman warriors, the student body cascaded across the campus, pouring out of the school, dropping everything, racing to take possession of the football field.

Inside his office Mr. Cooper watched in frustration.

"We've got to stop them!" he said.

But nobody could stop the rush of students now.

Elizabeth ran behind them, furiously taking notes on her steno pad about what was now the most exciting story ever to hit campus. And there was Todd, right in the middle of it all. By the time she got to the field, a group of angry kids had cornered Lila Fowler and Bruce Patman, the children of the two families involved.

"Hey, Fowler, what's with you?" Winston Egbert demanded of Lila. "Isn't your father rich enough already?"

"You leave my father out of this!" Lila screamed.

"A factory—how gross." Bruce Patman sneered. "That's all the Fowlers think of—grubby newcomers!"

"Listen to Mr. Two-Face," spat Winston.

"Yeah, your father wants some look-but-don't-touch *garden*," said Emily Mayer.

"Watch your face, Emily," Bruce said. "A garden would be an improvement over this mud shop. Besides, all the practice in the world won't help those lousy Gladiators!"

"You're a traitor, Patman!" somebody yelled.

"Where's your school spirit?" Jessica yelled at him.

"Aw, save it, Wakefield!"

"You and your family don't care about Sweet Valley High. You're a disgrace!" Jessica yelled.

"Hey, when it comes to having a disgrace in the family, Jessica Wakefield, just consider your dear sister, the pub crawler. And I do mean crawler!"

Elizabeth was taking notes when she heard it, and her face went bright red. Instantly she felt all eyes on her.

"You leave my sister out of this!" Jessica yelled.

"Why should we?" said Lila Fowler. "You're all treating Bruce and me like we're lepers! I thought you were a friend of mine, Jessica Wakefield."

"Lila, I am, but—"

"But, my backside," said Bruce. "And when it comes to a disgraceful family, Wakefield, how about your father and Marianna West—that trampy broad he's fooling around with."

"Now, just a minute," Elizabeth said, stepping forward. "Marianna West works for my father's law firm."

"Yeah? Where? On the couch, maybe?" Bruce sneered.

"You liar!"

Bruce laughed. "Sure! Your father spends all his time running around with a sexy woman, and you call that 'working for the firm.' "

"They're working together—to stop *you*," Elizabeth shouted.

"Yeah, yeah, yeah! Go put it in the paper!"

"Never mind that," Todd was saying, pushing his way to the front. "We're interested in saving the field. I think that's enough out of you," he told Bruce.

"OK," Ken shouted, climbing up onto the bleacher seats and addressing them all. "Are we giving up the field?"

"*No!*" came the roaring response.

"Are they putting up a factory?"

"*No!*"

"A garden?"

"*No!*"

"Come on, everybody," Jessica shouted. "The Gladiator cheer!"

She leaped down onto the track and led everybody in a Sweet Valley fight song.

Elizabeth frantically took notes, watching Todd from the corner of her eye.

This was the biggest story she had ever been given, but still Elizabeth kept hearing the hateful words Bruce Patman had flung out about her father and Marianna West.

Suddenly, as if seeing a missing puzzle piece falling into place, Elizabeth remembered the day the previous week when she'd accidentally walked into her parents' room while they were in the midst of an argument. Not an argument, really. They weren't shouting at each other or anything like that. It was more of a heated discussion. Her mother had seemed tense, and her father had worn an uncharacteristic frown.

She'd only caught the tail end of their conversation, but it had brought a sour taste to her mouth nevertheless.

"I never *said* my work was more important than yours," Ned Wakefield had argued in a voice straining to remain patient. "What I said was that it would be *nice* if we saw more of you. . . ."

It might have been just a minor complaint. Their mother had been working longer hours than usual lately, due to a special design project

97

she was involved in. But the incident bothered Elizabeth because her parents almost never argued. The thought of anything coming between them struck her like a sudden blow. What if the argument was just the tip of an iceberg named Marianna West? *No,* Elizabeth told herself, *my imagination is running away with me again. It can't be true. It just can't.*

Ten

Elizabeth was almost finished taking notes and ready to head back to the *Oracle* office when it happened. There he was, suddenly, right in front of her, face to face, and there was no possibility of ignoring him.

"Hi, Todd."

"Liz," said Todd, his face lighting up. "Hey, isn't this something?"

"Yeah! I'm covering it for *The Oracle*."

"Wow, Liz, this is a big story. I always knew you'd be a great reporter."

"Really?"

"Sure."

Todd looked away then, as though remembering something, and fell silent.

"I was just heading back to school," Elizabeth said hopefully.

"Yeah? I'm going back, too."

They might have made up then and there, Elizabeth thought later, except that suddenly Jessica came running over.

"Todd!"

"Hi, Jess," he said.

"I want to talk to you. It's terribly important," she gushed.

"Oh—sure," Todd said.

Elizabeth walked away as quickly as she could. She thought she heard Todd call her, but she kept on going, across the campus to the *Oracle* office. It was the longest walk of her life.

Inside the office at last, Elizabeth sat at the typewriter and plunged into writing the story. It was like a doctor's prescription—it shut out all the pain and longing.

Write, she told herself. *Keep on writing. Forget everything else.*

Todd watched with a sense of loss as Elizabeth walked away. He'd had a precious moment when everything might have been set right, and he'd let it slip away.

Somebody was talking at him. It was Jessica Wakefield.

"Earth to Todd Wilkins," she was saying with a slight trace of irritation. He was such a hunk and just about the nicest guy at Sweet Valley High, but sometimes he seemed so dense!

"What did you say, Jessica?"

They were strolling along back toward the school again, and Jessica kept the pace leisurely. She wanted Todd to herself this time.

"Liz was sure in a hurry," he said.

"Yes," Jessica said slowly. "She's upset these days."

"I guess she would be," Todd said. "Living down a stunt like that isn't easy."

"That's what I wanted to talk to you about," Jessica began. "It's just terrible, what's happening. What kids are saying."

"But it's all true, Jessica! I'd give anything to find out it wasn't."

"Oh, Todd," Jessica whimpered, and she ran a few steps to a bench on the lawn and collapsed onto it. Todd was beside her in a minute.

"What's the matter, Jessica?"

Jessica was crying with abandon, holding her face in her hands and sobbing. Her shoulders shook. She wouldn't look at him.

"Hey—Jess!"

Todd sat beside her and pulled her close, holding her against him as she cried. "Come on, now. It can't be that bad."

"Oh, Todd! I just can't stand it, what people are saying about Elizabeth. I love her more than anything in the world. I can't let her be treated like this."

Jessica looked up into Todd's concerned face, into his wonderfully tender brown eyes, and her heart fluttered.

"Todd, it could have happened to anyone! It's not fair! Why, it could have happened to *me*."

"Come on, Jessica. It didn't just happen. She knew what she was doing."

Jessica took a deep breath. "Todd, I can't let this go on. Elizabeth is my sister. I love her! Todd—it wasn't Elizabeth at Kelly's."

"It wasn't?"

"No. Todd, it was me!"

"What?"

"Yes. Me. My sister is *not* going to be blamed for this thing. It's not fair."

Jessica was totally amazed at what happened next. Todd Wilkins stared deeply into her eyes for a long moment, then slowly shook his head as though in wonder.

"I've never heard anything so noble," he finally said.

"What?"

"You'd take the blame for your sister? Jessica, I don't think I've ever known how truly special you are until this moment."

"But, Todd—"

Todd pulled her close, holding her tightly in

102

his strong arms for what seemed an eternity. Then he gently kissed her. He didn't even hear the whistles and yells from the students who saw the whole thing, right in the center of the campus in the middle of the afternoon.

Jessica sat there, stunned. Never in her wildest dreams had she imagined that telling the truth could be so rewarding.

"Jessica, you're wonderful," Todd said.

"Todd, you're the greatest guy I've ever met, do you know that?"

"Listen! I'm taking you to the Phi Ep dance!"

"What?"

"That is, if you want to go with me."

"Want to? Oh, Todd!" And she was around his neck once more. "I want it more than anything in the world."

The first thing Elizabeth heard about as she left the *Oracle* office, was about the Big Love Scene between Todd and Jessica on the bench in the center of campus.

"Wow," Winston Egbert hooted, stopping Elizabeth as she came out of the school building. "The temperature went up about fifty degrees here a little while ago."

"What happened, Winston?"

"A certain beautiful cheerleader and a certain handsome basketball captain went into a clinch right out in front of the world, and the mercury soared!"

"Oh," said Elizabeth. Her heart ached.

"I thought Todd was going after you, but now I see it's Jessica. Boy, talk about showing your feelings in public."

"Why are you so surprised, Winston? You of all people. You've been in love with Jessica since fifth grade. She's fantastic, and you know it."

"Oh, I *know* she is, but so are you!"

"Oh, well . . ."

"Who are you going to the dance with?"

"Good question, Winston."

They walked down the steps. There, at the foot, Bruce Patman was gliding up to them in his black Porsche.

"Well, well, well," Bruce said to Elizabeth. "If it isn't Roadhouse Rhoda."

Elizabeth froze.

"Listen, I never thought you were such a fast number until now. But from what I hear, I've decided you're my type. I'd like to take you to the dance."

"Is that so?" Elizabeth snapped.

"Sure. I can't stand most of these wimpy girls. We can put in an appearance at the dance, then head for someplace where we can have some real fun."

All the pent-up fury suddenly burst from her.

All the anguish and the hurt and the pain caused by the snickering and whispering and innuendos spilled out.

"Bruce Patman, I'd rather stay home for the rest of my life than go anywhere with you! But, as a matter of fact, I have a date."

"Yeah? Who with?"

"Me!"

Elizabeth spun around.

There stood Winston Egbert, looking shocked at the sound of his own voice.

"You?" Bruce Patman laughed. "You, the joke of the school?"

"Yeah? Well, maybe I'm a joke, but you're an insult."

Bruce Patman started to climb out of the car, his face flushed and mean. "You stupid nothing, I'll fold you up and stuff you in the trash can!"

Elizabeth stepped between them. "Never mind, Bruce. It happens to be true. Win and I are going to the dance."

She linked her arm in Winston's and led him away, leaving Bruce Patman sitting in his car with his mouth open in astonishment.

"Listen, I'm sorry," Winston said when they were out of earshot from Bruce. "I just got so mad! I won't hold you to it."

"Wait a minute. What is this, Win? Are you standing me up?"

"Huh?"

"You asked me for a date, didn't you?"

"Well—I—aw, Liz, I just couldn't help it."

"Pick me up at seven-thirty, OK?"

Winston Egbert stared at the beautiful, popular, intelligent Elizabeth Wakefield and almost fainted.

"OK!" he said, astounded, then turned and raced madly across campus, screaming like a deranged chimpanzee.

For the first time in ages, Elizabeth laughed long and hard. Then she turned her steps toward home. She would have fun with Winston at the dance, she really would. It was difficult not to laugh when he was around.

She felt a lot better now and walked along jauntily. She even began whistling. It wasn't until she reached her own street that her steps faltered and she wondered if she was whistling for some reason other than happiness. Maybe, just maybe, it kept her from hearing her own painful thoughts.

Eleven

Elizabeth dragged herself through the house and into the kitchen. She pulled a carton of milk out of the refrigerator and poured a glassful. As she drank, she chanted inwardly, *I am happy for Jess . . . I am happy for Jess. . . .But I'm so miserable I could die!*

Just then the front door slammed shut, and Elizabeth heard Jessica shout, "Lizzie! Lizzie! Oh, Lizzie, you're not going to believe this!"

Jessica burst into the room, and it was the Fourth of July, Christmas morning, and Mardi Gras all rolled into one ecstatic, beautiful, blond sixteen-year-old.

"I told him, Liz, I told him everything. I told him that it was me with Rick Andover at Kelly's—and he *still* invited me to the dance!"

"You told him, Jess? He knows it wasn't me?"

"I told him *everything*, and he forgave me! He has got to be the most wonderful boy in a hundred and thirty-seven states!"

Elizabeth was sure that something inside her died just then. If Todd knew it was Jessica at Kelly's and still asked her to the dance—well, she knew where that left her. Nowhere. She would go to the dance with Winston, have a wonderful time, get busy on her writing, and forget about Todd. *How in the world are you going to do that?* she asked herself.

"That's sensational, Jess. You're going to have a terrific time. I hear Todd is a great dancer."

"He's great at everything, I think!" Jessica was bubbling over. "Where's Mom? I can't wait to tell her all about this."

"She's going to be late. An appointment, I think."

"Again?" Jessica pouted. "That makes three nights in a row! I thought mothers were supposed to stay home and fix dinner once in a while!"

Elizabeth wondered how her sister could possibly descend from cloud nine with Todd Wilkins to the pits of depression so fast—and simply because she had to do a little thing like help fix dinner.

"Mom told us this morning that she was going to be late, Jess," Elizabeth said patiently, trying to hide her unhappiness and control her temper all at the same time.

"Well, it's not fair," Jessica complained, storming around the kitchen. "She has ruined my day, totally and absolutely!"

Elizabeth stared at her sister in amazement. Had Jessica flipped out? How could anyone ruin a day that included a dance invitation from Todd Wilkins? She imagined how she would feel if Todd had asked her. She would be so far off the ground she'd need a pilot's license. The thought of Todd's arms around her, the two of them dancing to slow, romantic music, made her knees so weak she had to clutch the counter with both hands to keep standing. Then she thought of how the evening would end—they'd be alone, totally alone . . . his arms would hold her close to him . . . his lips—

"Liz! You haven't heard a word I've said," Jessica accused.

"What?" said Elizabeth, reluctantly coming out of her daydream.

"My very own sister is turning into an airhead right before my eyes. I was *trying* to find out what time Mom will be home. *If* she's coming home at all. She's practically never home anymore. Of course, if you're too busy to talk to me, just say so, Elizabeth." Jessica was working herself up to the rage of the century.

Elizabeth turned toward her sister. One look at Jessica's unhappy face was all it took.

"Oh, Jess, I'm sorry," she said, giving her a

quick hug. "This hasn't been a world-class day for me. You have every right to be happy. I want you to know that I'm really pleased for you." *After all,* she thought with just a trace of bitterness, *somebody in this family should be happy.*

"Liz! Stop it, Lizzie! You're doing it again."

"I'm listening, I'm listening. I swear it! Why is it so important to know when Mom's going to get home?"

"I want to tell her about this sensational day. And I absolutely have to talk her into getting me that perfect—oh, Lizzie, you should see it— perfect dress at the mall." The sunshine was definitely back in Jessica's face and voice.

"Tell me all about it," Elizabeth said, then sighed, *"while* you're setting the table. Let me check out the freezer to see what I can toss into the microwave."

"Well, it's blue. It's slinky—"

"Don't forget the table, Jess."

Jessica glared at her sister's back for a moment but decided she'd better set the table if she expected Elizabeth to listen to her.

"Did I say blue—and slinky?" As Elizabeth nodded, Jessica continued. "It has a handkerchief hemline and—wait till you hear this, Lizzie— spaghetti straps and a neckline *so* low Todd will be panting."

"Sounds like a case of overkill to me, Jess, and as a man, I feel sorry for the intended victim."

Both girls spun around in surprise. Steven was standing just inside the archway between the kitchen and dining room.

"Steve!" they chorused.

"I'm starved. Is there enough of whatever that's going to be for one more?" he asked, gesturing at the frozen food package Elizabeth was opening.

"Sure," she said. "It's just the three of us for dinner tonight. But I thought you—I mean, aren't you going out tonight?"

"No," he answered flatly.

The twins exchanged worried looks.

"It's probably a good thing Mom and Dad aren't here," he said bitterly. "I'm definitely not up to a repeat of last weekend's third degree!"

"I'm sure they don't mean to grill you, Steve, they're just concerned and—"

"For Pete's sake, Liz, not you, too! Why can't *everyone* in this house mind their own business!"

"This family has got to be the biggest bummer in five hundred and thirty-seven cities!" Jessica exploded. "Boring! Boring! Boring!" She stomped around the room, with the full attention of her brother and sister. Then she whirled, pointing a finger at Elizabeth.

"You," she sputtered, "act like you're a candidate for the funny farm. All you do is mope, mope, mope! And *you!*" She suddenly shifted to Steven. "What a ray of sunshine you are!

And on top of everything else, I was humiliated in front of every single person in school because my very own father is having an affair with that—that *woman!*"

Steven's head snapped up, and he glared at Jessica. "What are you talking about?"

"Oh, Steve," she cried, "it's all over school, all over town. Dad has been with Marianna West almost every single night, and Mom acts like she doesn't care at all. They're headed for the divorce courts! What's going to happen to us?"

"Stop it, Jess," Elizabeth broke in. "Just because Bruce Patman shot off his mouth doesn't mean that any of it is true."

"Any of what?" Steven wanted to know. "Will one of you please tell me what's going on around here?"

"Well, Dad *has* been spending a lot of evenings with Ms. West," Elizabeth said, groping for the right words. "He says he's helping her with a case."

"He *says*," put in Jessica.

"But you two don't believe him?"

"No!" Jessica blurted out.

It took Elizabeth a few moments longer to speak. "I want to believe him, Steve, but things have been sort of strange around here lately, and—I just don't know."

"Does Mom seem worried or upset?" he asked.

"No, and that's the trouble!" Jessica raged. "How can she be so blind? Dad is so good-looking—at least for a man his age—and Marianna is kind of attractive, if you like the flashy type. Of course they're having an affair. What else are we supposed to think?"

"You could try believing Dad, for starters," Steve said angrily. He walked restlessly around the room. "Dad has never lied to us. If he says he's helping her with a case, that's what he's doing."

"Isn't that just like a man!" Jessica spat. "You always stick up for each other. You're just as bad as Dad. As a matter of fact, you're just like him. You *both* have bad taste in women!"

It would have taken a machete to slice through the tension in the room. Jessica and Steven sat glaring at each other.

Obviously trying to control his rage, Steven spoke in a low, cold voice. "You've got five seconds to explain that crack, Jessica!"

Jessica had spoken without thinking, not unusual for her, and she was afraid of the consequences. She had never seen Steven so angry with her before. She had to say something, quickly.

"Steve, I meant—I mean, I didn't mean—how can you stand there glaring at me so hatefully? This was supposed to be my happy day, and now you're trying to ruin it!" Jessica buried her face in her arms, sobbing helplessly.

"You selfish little twerp," Steven said, glaring at Jessica.

Elizabeth jumped in quickly between them. "Steve, please, you don't understand," she pleaded.

"Don't you ever get tired of defending her?" Steve snapped.

"You don't understand what kind of a day it's been for Jess and me. You don't know what people said about Dad." Elizabeth was getting desperate. She had to make Steven see. "Steve, we know! We know about you and—her."

That stopped him. He looked at her for a long moment. "You know about me and *her*? What's that supposed to mean?" he demanded.

Elizabeth took a deep breath and plunged in. "Steve, we know everything. We weren't snooping around or trying to butt in, honest!"

"I'm sorry, too, Steve," Jessica added. "I shouldn't have blurted it like that. But you and Betsy Martin—it can't be. She's trash."

"*Betsy* Martin? What are you talking about? I'm in love with *Tricia* Martin."

"Tricia? You mean Betsy's sister?" Elizabeth asked, stunned.

"Yeah, Tricia." Saying her name conjured up memories for Steven. Lovely Tricia with her strawberry-blond hair, her sweet nature, everything he wanted in this world.

"That's wonderful, Steve," Elizabeth said.

"Tricia is a terrific girl—one of the best! I'm so happy for you!"

"She's still a Martin," Jessica reminded him.

"Not to worry, Jess. Nothing important is going to happen between the *respected* Wakefield family and the low-life Martins. Basically because I blew it. Oh, boy, did I blow it!"

Steven's unhappy story spilled out. As long as he and Tricia were alone together at Tricia's house, everything had been wonderful. But gradually Tricia had concluded that Steven didn't want to be seen in public with her, that he was ashamed to be associated with her family. That was why he never took her anywhere. "You're a snob, Steven Wakefield!" she had said.

"She's right, too," Steven said to the twins. "And now I've lost Tricia—forever."

As Elizabeth stared at her brother, she was filled with despair. She recalled the old saying about trouble coming in threes. She counted:

I've lost Todd.

Steve's lost Tricia.

Mom losing Dad would make it three.

Jessica, she noted coolly, was the only one who had managed to escape unscathed so far.

Twelve

"You're not serious. You absolutely cannot be going with Winston Egbert!" screeched Jessica as she stood in the middle of Elizabeth's room. "I can't believe my own sister dating that clown!"

It was the evening before the dance, but Jessica had been so preoccupied with her own plans for the big night that she hadn't heard about Elizabeth and Winston until an hour earlier at dinner.

"I don't understand why you're so upset about it, Jess," Elizabeth said as she sat on her bed, her history book in her lap. "Win's a nice guy. He's really funny. And even if he's not handsome, he doesn't have three heads, for heaven's sake!"

"But he's not romantic, Lizzie," Jessica pointed out.

"That suits me just fine. I can relax and have a good time without worrying about groping hands and fighting someone off at the front door." Elizabeth sighed, knowing Todd would never be so crude. A good-night kiss from him would be nothing short of heaven.

Jessica heard the sigh and saw the faraway look on her sister's face.

"Lizzie," she began in what she hoped was a casual tone, "are you going with Winston because you really want to, or because nobody else asked you?"

Elizabeth hesitated to tell her sister about Bruce Patman's invitation. She doubted that Jessica would see it her way. At the time it had made her furious, but now it seemed kind of funny. The look on his face had been priceless. Nobody, but *nobody*, turned Bruce Patman down for a date.

"Actually, Jess, someone else did ask me first. Bruce Patman."

"Bruce Patman!" Jessica squealed. "Liz Wakefield, how dare you sit there calmly and tell me Bruce asked you out as if it weren't important! You're incredible! No—you must be dead! No girl alive would turn Bruce down. He's handsome, Liz. He is sooooo rich. And he drives that awesome Porsche!" Jessica stood there, hands on hips, glaring down at her sister. Jessica would never say no to Bruce. She thought for a minute of how it would be to arrive at a dance with him. Once in a while it seemed to Jessica that Bruce was on the verge of asking her out, but it hadn't happened, *yet*.

"Are you saying you wish you were going to the dance with Bruce instead of Todd?" Elizabeth challenged.

"Of course not. Why in the world would you think that? Todd is terribly good-looking, and he's so sweet. I just wish he didn't drive that gross excuse for a car. Bruce's Porsche is so—so . . . I mean, it's a *Porsche*."

"Let's get off the subject of Bruce Patman, *please*." Elizabeth got up off the bed and walked over to her table, where she picked up some notes. "Right now I've got to study for tomorrow's history quiz."

"Yeah, OK, I'm going." Jessica hesitated at the door. "Just one thing, Liz."

Elizabeth looked up from the notes.

"Are you sure it's all right? You know, about Todd and me and the dance?" There was genuine concern in Jessica's blue-green eyes.

"Jess, I don't know what you're—"

"Please tell me the truth. Sometimes you get a funny faraway look when Todd's name is mentioned. I wondered if you sort of liked him. If it makes you unhappy, I won't go out with him, I swear! I'll stay home tomorrow." By this time, Jessica was on the other side of the table, clutching Elizabeth's hands. She really seemed concerned.

A flood of love for her sister washed over Elizabeth. She knew how important the dance was for Jessica. She couldn't, she *wouldn't* spoil it for her.

"Who's being an airhead now, Jess? We're both going to that dance, and we'll have a sensational time! The Wakefield sisters are going to be *so* terrific!"

"How terrific are we going to be, Liz?" asked Jessica, happy once again.

"Get out of here, you idiot," said Elizabeth, grabbing a small pillow and aiming it at Jessica.

As soon as Jessica left the room, the smile left Elizabeth's face. *Will it really be such a terrific night?* she asked herself, tears filling her eyes.

"Thanks, Jess. Thanks a bunch," Elizabeth called from the bathroom that adjoined the twins' rooms. She was wrapped in a towel.

"You're welcome, but for what?" Jessica shouted over the whir of the hair dryer.

"For leaving me the steamiest bathroom in the entire state and exactly thirty seconds of hot water!" Elizabeth hollered back.

"Oops," Jessica said, poking her head into the room. "I'm sorry. Would you believe I got carried away?"

"It wouldn't be the first time."

"What do you think?" Jessica gave her golden mane a toss. "I mean, be totally honest. Is my hair OK?"

"Ummm, let me look." She circled Jessica. Every hair was exactly where it should be—perfect.

"Sad, Jess. It's really sad."

"What?" screeched Jessica. "What are you saying?"

"I just thought, you know—poor Vidal Sassoon on the unemployment line because you're better than he is."

Elizabeth fell on the bed laughing. "Gotcha, Jess!" she shouted triumphantly.

"Hi, Mrs. Wakefield. I'm Todd Wilkins. I'm here to pick up Li—Jessica, I mean, for the dance."

"Come in, Todd. It's nice to meet you. Jess will be down in a minute." She ushered him into the large, airy living room.

The doorbell rang again.

"Excuse me, Todd, this seems to be a busy night."

Alice Wakefield brought Winston Egbert into the room. "You two know each other, I assume?"

"Sure. Hi, Winston."

"Hey, Todd! How about the two of us,

huh? Escorting the beautiful Wakefield sisters. Wow!"

Todd and Winston stood in the living room waiting for Elizabeth and Jessica. Gone were the school uniforms of jeans and T-shirts. Both wore neatly pressed cords, shirts and ties, and sport coats.

Elizabeth was the first to come down the stairs, and both Todd and Winston watched her descend. The white strapless dress was perfect with her tanned skin and blond hair. She kept the bright smile on her face even when she saw Todd. Why couldn't she and Winston have been gone before Todd arrived? she asked herself.

Winston nervously looked toward the stairs as if he were expecting someone else. Then he nearly threw himself at Elizabeth's feet. Spreading his arms wide and looking upward, he declared, "I've died. I've died and gone to heaven!" Getting up, he made a grand bow. "Princess Elizabeth, you are totally—totally—that's what you are, Liz Wakefield—totally!"

Elizabeth found herself laughing so hard she was nearly in tears. "Win Egbert, you are totally crazy! And if you make me cry and ruin my eye makeup, I'll kill you! So help me, I'll kill you!"

Alice Wakefield was smiling that particular smile every mother does when her child is happy.

Todd Wilkins, however, was not smiling. His

expression was a strange mixture of anger and sadness.

Jessica, out of sight but not out of earshot in the upstairs hall, was also not smiling. *How dare that idiot Win Egbert spoil my entrance?* she asked herself. He was acting like an airhead, and she would never speak to him again.

"My lady, our coach awaits!" Winston said as he opened the door with a flourish.

Elizabeth laughed. "I knew it. You're taking me to the dance in a pumpkin!"

Winston was still chuckling as he followed her outside. "Close," he said. "It's orange, and it doesn't go very fast."

They both dissolved into giggles as he led her over to the orange VW bug parked in the driveway.

Alice Wakefield was still laughing when the door closed. "Those two are really too much, aren't they, Todd?"

"Yeah, too much," he answered somewhat sourly.

Just then Jessica made her entrance. She looked nothing less than sensational. The blue dress with its delicate straps and full skirt showed off her slim body and gorgeous legs.

"Hello, Todd," she said softly, her mouth curved in a lovely smile.

"Hi, Jess," he answered. "You look nice— really very pretty."

Nice! she screamed silently. *Three hours of working on my nails, my hair, my makeup and I look "very pretty"? Whatever happened to gorgeous?*

"Thanks, Todd." *Maybe he's not good with words,* she thought. But she knew from the other day that he was good with kissing—and there certainly would be more kisses that evening!

The Droids were playing loudly, and the lights were bright as Jessica and Todd arrived at the dance.

"Oh, Todd, isn't it wonderful?" She wrapped her arm around his. "Look at the hearts!" she cried, pointing out the red and silver 3-D foil hearts with PBA on one side and PE on the other. "It's so romantic. A sweetheart dance!" She sighed.

"Yeah, it's nice, Jess," he answered, his eyes scanning the room.

Jessica wasn't sure how many more *nices* she could take. Something was going wrong with her evening, and it had better stop right now!

"Todd, look! There's Cara Walker. Let's go talk to her. And there's Lila Fowler. And poor Bruce Patman came stag tonight."

"*Poor* Bruce Patman?"

"Oh, I didn't mean *poor*," she bubbled. "It's just that he's one of the many guys who invited

Liz to the dance tonight. My sister is soooo popular, Todd."

"So I've heard, Jess, so I've heard." His voice tightened. "We're here to dance, right? Let's dance!"

The Droids were playing a hard, driving number as Todd pulled Jessica onto the dance floor. They were both great dancers, and they looked so terrific together that the other couples moved out of their way. Jessica danced around Todd, her dress flaring out as she twirled. Her beautiful tanned legs caught every boy's eyes. Then she and Todd really started getting into the music, in a very sexy way. As the number came to an end, the crowd erupted with applause, whistles, and cries for more. Jessica threw her arms around Todd and hugged him. She never noticed Todd staring across the room at a set of identical blue-green eyes.

"Hey, Liz, remember me? Your wonderful date-type person?" Winston said.

"Oh, Win!"

"Yeah, good old forgettable Win. How about a dance, Liz? Nobody's going to desert the floor when I do my thing, but I promise not to break all your toes."

"Let's go, Win," Elizabeth said, knowing she

couldn't spend the whole evening watching Jessica and Todd.

"We seem to be here with the wrong people, Liz," he said as they moved somewhat awkwardly around the floor. Contrary to Winston's promise, Elizabeth had to be very careful about her toes.

"Huh?"

"Well," he explained, "you're watching Todd, and he's practically got his eyes glued on you."

"Really, Win? You really think he's watching me?"

"Really, really, really, Liz. The only thing wrong is that your gorgeous sister is watching him, too. I wish she were watching me."

"Oh, Win. You're still loyal to Jessica, huh?"

"You'd better believe it," he said in a serious tone Elizabeth had never heard him use before. Then suddenly he made a hideous face that cracked her up. He was back to being the clown again.

"You want to know the sort of girl people fix me up with?" he asked. "It goes like this: 'Win, have I got a girl for you! What a personality!' That always means two hundred and fifty pounds and two-foot-five! I have to put her hamburger on the floor so she can reach it."

"But, Win," Elizabeth said, laughing, "looks aren't everything."

"Yeah, I know. I'm no prize package, either,

right?" He grinned affably. "Hey, Enid and Ronnie are waving at us. Let's go over and say hello, OK?"

As they made their way around the dancers, Elizabeth commented, "I don't think Ronnie has left her side all evening. He's certainly protective."

"Yeah. I think he was a Doberman in a former life," Winston cracked.

A set of brown eyes followed Elizabeth's every move, a fact that did not go unnoticed by Jessica, who was rapidly reaching the boiling point. Her evening was going right down the tubes, and it was all Todd's fault. She had done everything—and with Jessica, that was plenty—to keep his eyes on her. Except for that one sensational dance, he had hardly looked at her.

No guy—not even Todd Wilkins—could take Jessica Wakefield to a dance and treat her like a piece of furniture. He wasn't going to get away with it, she vowed.

Later that night Elizabeth sat on her bed and sighed with relief that the long evening was finally over. A bunch of the kids had gone out for pizza after the dance, but she had persuaded Winston to bring her home. She knew she couldn't bear seeing Todd and Jessica together one minute longer. What were they doing now? she wondered. Were they kissing? Were they . . . ? *Stop torturing yourself!*

At that very moment, Todd was saying good night to Jessica at the front door.

Nervously he shifted his weight from one foot to the other. "Jessica," he finally mumbled, "thanks. Thanks a lot. It's been a—a really great evening."

Not yet it hasn't, Jessica thought. *But it could still end up great.*

She placed her hands lightly on his shoulders and swayed close to him.

"Oh, Todd," she breathed, closing her eyes and raising her face for a kiss.

But the kiss, when it came, was nothing like what she'd expected. Jessica's heart went into a tailspin. A kiss on the cheek! Like he was her *brother*, for cripe's sake! She'd never been so humiliated in her entire life!

"Yeah, really great, Jess. See you at school."

And he was gone.

"You creep!" Jessica said aloud as she stood there by herself. "Todd Wilkins, I swear I'll get even with you if it's the last thing I ever do!"

Elizabeth reached out to turn off her light but stopped when she heard the front door close.

Jessica was home. *I suppose I'll have to listen to every dreamy detail.*

Jessica stuck her head into the room. "Can we talk for a minute, Liz?"

"Sure, Jess. Tell me all about it. I'll bet you had one fabulous time tonight!"

"Fabulous?"

"Well, of course. An evening with Todd. Good-looking, good dancer, super-nice guy. What more could you want?"

Jessica suddenly knew how she was going to get even with Todd. That "nice guy" image was about to be destroyed.

"Oh, Liz, it was so awful!" Jessica's eyes filled with tears.

"Awful? What are you talking about, Jess?"

"I thought he liked me, Lizzie," she said between sobs. "I thought he respected me and everything!"

"Jessie, what happened?"

"Oh, Liz, I can't. I can't tell you!" Jessica collapsed, covering her face with her hands. "I'm—I'm too ashamed."

Elizabeth put her arm around Jessica's shoulder. "It's all right, Jess. You can tell me anything, you know that."

"Maybe I should tell you." Jessica sniffled. "You really should be warned about him. You might go out with him sometime, and I'd just never forgive myself if I didn't tell you what the *real* Todd Wilkins is like."

"What did he do?"

"That rat tried just about everything. The horrible thing was that I could hardly make him stop. I had to beg him and beg him to please stop!"

"Oh, no." Elizabeth moaned, squeezing Jessica's shoulder in sympathy. "I can't believe it."

"I know. I couldn't believe it either. I even remember saying to him as I was fighting him off that I couldn't believe it."

"And what did he do *then*?" Elizabeth asked, flushed with anger.

"I don't remember. But, oh, Liz, it was awful. He just wouldn't stop. His hands! Oh, God, they were everywhere. And—"

"Don't tell me any more. I've heard enough."

Jessica wiped away the tears with the back of her hand. "Lizzie, you're not mad at me for telling you, are you?" she asked. "I just didn't want you ever to be in that kind of situation. I wanted to protect you, Lizzie."

"Of course I'm not mad, Jess. Not at *you*, anyway," Elizabeth exploded. "How dare Todd Wilkins treat you that way? How dare he! I'll kill him—absolutely kill him!" she raged.

No need, Liz, Jessica said to herself. *I just took care of that myself.*

Thirteen

The knock on the door was soft but persistent.

"Steve?"

No answer. Ned Wakefield knocked again.

"I have to talk to you."

Mr. Wakefield turned the doorknob slowly. The room was in total darkness, although it was almost nine in the morning. He pulled up the shades and walked toward the bed, where his son was hidden under the blankets.

"Hey."

Steven didn't stir.

Ned Wakefield sat on the bed and poked the lump under the blankets. "I'm not going away, so you might as well come out."

The blanket fell away from his face, and Steven blinked at his father. There was a two-day beard on his face, and his eyes were bloodshot and swollen.

"You look terrible," said Mr. Wakefield.

Steven sat up on the side of the bed and held his face in his hands. "Why not? I feel terrible."

"Listen, Steve, I used to think my troubles would go away if I hid out long enough, too. But they won't."

"Thanks, Dr. Wakefield."

"You're welcome. Now, get up, shave, take a shower, and come on down. Let's talk."

"I thought you had an important case to work on."

"I have. Wakefield versus Wakefield. Up!"

Back downstairs, Alice Wakefield looked at her husband with concern. "Is he up?"

"He's coming down."

"Thank goodness."

They had known that Steven was depressed the last two weekends he had been home. This weekend was worse. Steven had been hiding in his bedroom for two days with no explanation. When he had not gone back to school Sunday night, Alice and Ned Wakefield had cornered the twins and demanded to know what was happening. It was like pulling teeth. Neither Elizabeth nor Jessica wanted to squeal on their older brother. But eventually the story about Tricia Martin had come out.

Steven looked much better when he came

131

downstairs. He sat down at the table, and his mother put orange juice in front of him, but he pushed it aside.

"Not hungry, Mom."

"Hmmm. This *must* be serious," his mother said lightly. She was rewarded with a glare that might have bored holes through a brick wall. "Sorry."

"Steve, let me tell you something," his father said. "Anything you're going through, *I* went through."

"Sure."

"Yeah—*sure*. And so did your mother."

"Mom?" That got his attention. "Aw, what do you mean. You two—"

"What?"

"Nothing."

"We never had a problem in our lives? Is that what you think?" said Mrs. Wakefield.

Steven picked up the glass of orange juice and sipped it. He felt uncomfortable talking about his mom and dad, especially now when there might be something going on with Marianna West.

"But never mind us," said his father. "What's all this about Tricia Martin?"

Steven sighed. "The twins told you? Oh, well. It doesn't matter anyway."

"Why'd you have to keep it a big secret?" Alice Wakefield asked. "Tricia's a lovely girl."

"Yeah, I know. But her family . . ."

Ned and Alice Wakefield exchanged glances. Tricia Martin's family was no bargain, and they knew it. Her father was the town drunk, and her sister Betsy had a horrible reputation. The mother had died of leukemia when the kids were little, which really had torn the family apart. It was all understandable, but that didn't make it any easier. And now Steven was mixed up with them. The question was, how seriously?

"Listen," Steven was saying, "this is really no big deal. Just forget it." He started to rise again, but his father's hand on his arm sat him back down.

"Steve, anything that's kept you hiding out for two days is important enough for me. How serious are you about Tricia?"

"Well, Dad, I think I'm in love with her. She's really terrific."

"And how does she feel about you?" Alice Wakefield asked.

Steven got up and paced around the kitchen. "She hates me! She'll never speak to me again. And it's all my fault. I don't deserve such a great girl."

The anguished tale then poured out of Steven Wakefield. He heaped abuse upon himself as he told them how he had pretended that her family's problems didn't matter. He loved her "anyway," he had told her, and he was above that sort of thing.

"She saw right through me," Steven said bitterly. "She saw the truth—a truth I didn't even realize—that I was ashamed of her family. That I didn't consider her good enough for me but that I would accept her out of the goodness of my heart. What an idiot I was! Now it's all over. She never wants to see me again. And I don't blame her. I'm just miserable."

"Have you told Tricia what you just told us?" said his mother.

Steven stopped pacing. Slowly he sat down at the table. He poured some coffee and sipped it. He shook his head.

"I couldn't do that, Mom."

"Why?"

"It would be too—I'd sound like such a jerk."

"Is it the truth, Steven?"

"That I'm a jerk? Yes, it's true."

"No, no—that you didn't realize what you were doing."

"Yes," Steven said slowly. "That's true."

"Do you still love Tricia?"

"Oh, yes." Not a moment's hesitation.

"Then go and tell her exactly what you told us."

"It's the only thing you can do," Ned Wakefield urged.

Steven looked at the table for a moment, and

when he spoke, he couldn't face his parents. He asked quietly, "What do you think of my being involved with the Martins?"

"You're not involved with the Martins, Steven. You're involved with Tricia."

"You don't mind?"

Ned and Alice Wakefield glanced at each other.

"Steven, you can't judge a person by his or her family," said Mrs. Wakefield. "I won't pretend that the Martins don't make me uneasy. But if you love Tricia, then you've got to fight for her. She's *Tricia* Martin—not Betsy, not her father."

Steven was up on his feet again, pacing. "You're sure you approve of Tricia, Mom? Dad?"

"Steven, it's whether *you* approve of her," Ned Wakefield said. "Follow your own judgment—as well as your heart."

Steven searched his father's face anxiously and then his mother's, looking for a clue to the pain and suffering they might be undergoing. Was this long-lasting, seemingly warm and solid marriage on the verge of destruction? Steven wished he could tell, but it was impossible. Whatever their problems, they were united to help him. Steven felt love racing through him, and he suddenly grabbed his mother in a bear hug.

"Hey—"

"I love you, Mom!"

"I love you, too, Steve."

"You, too, Dad," he said, grabbing his father's hand.

And then Steven vaulted through the kitchen door, dashed out the front door, and was gone, on his way to Tricia Martin's house.

Steven drove up to the Martin's saggy-roofed ranch house, a neglected old place that badly needed a paint job and general cleanup. As he approached the door, he could hear Tricia coaxing her father into his room.

"Come on, Pop. Lie down and get some sleep. You'll feel a lot better," Tricia said.

Steven opened the door and entered quietly. Tricia was returning to the living room.

"Steve!" she gasped. "What are you doing here? I thought I'd made it clear—we have nothing more to say to one another."

"There is one more thing I have to say, Tricia," Steven said softly. "I'm sorry. I'm sorry I acted like such a jerk. You were right. I *was* being patronizing, but I was too stupid to realize it. Can you forgive me, Trish, for being a complete fool? I love you. I love you so much."

"Oh, Steve," Trish said. "I love you, too."

She was so beautiful and fragile at that moment, Steven thought, her brown eyes shining, her hair floating about her oval face in a red-gold cloud.

With tears streaming down their faces, Steven and Tricia shared a long, tender kiss.

"I'm sorry, sweetheart, I'm so sorry," Steven said softly, planting gentle kisses on her eyes, her nose, and her forehead.

"Tricia! Tricia, come here," a voice called from the other room.

"My father needs me, Steve. I have to go to him."

"Can we talk later? There's so much I want to tell you. How about a long conversation over clams and a shake at the Dairi Burger tonight?" Steven asked, holding her face in his hands.

Tricia beamed a radiant smile. "OK, see you around eight." She rushed into her father's room as a very happy and relieved Steven Wakefield let himself out the front door.

The evening had been beautiful, Steven mused as he drove home after dropping Tricia off. His thoughts swirled pleasantly around her lovely image. And then, as though to cap off the evening perfectly, he spotted his father's rust-brown LTD just ahead of him. It would be fun to follow his dad home and thank him for helping him with what had seemed a hopeless mess. Steven turned on some soft music and cruised quietly along, dreaming happy dreams. He wasn't ready for the turn his father suddenly made into a side street.

Without really thinking, Steven turned also and followed the car. Only then did he notice that there was someone else in the car with his father.

Marianna West!

Steven didn't know what to do. He certainly hadn't planned to spy on his father. But there he was, following his father and Marianna— and wondering what in heaven's name was going on. It was too late, he realized, for them to be coming home from work.

The LTD began to slow down.

Steven slowed down, too. He couldn't pass them now. He slid his car into the shadows of a hedge along the drive and parked there.

The LTD pulled into a driveway and stopped. Marianna West got out. So did Steven's father. They were laughing together about something as they walked toward Marianna's white-shuttered house.

"Oh, no." Steven moaned. He didn't *want* to believe it, but the evidence was too glaring to ignore.

He sat in the car for a long time, waiting for his father to come out. He listened to at least a dozen songs on the radio, without hearing any of the music, before he finally gave up and drove home. Everyone was asleep when he got there.

Steven paused outside his parents' bedroom door on his way upstairs. The lights were off, so he knew his mother wasn't sitting up worrying. *Poor Mom*, he thought, *if she only knew . . .*

Steven crawled into bed, but he didn't want to go to sleep. He wanted to be awake when his father arrived home—*if* he came home at all.

Fourteen

Elizabeth couldn't remember a time when life had been such a mess. Everything was in a shambles. Her father was chasing around after another woman, and her mother was blind to it. The money-grubbing Fowlers were grabbing the Sweet Valley High Gladiators' football field away from them just when they had a really terrific team. And who was trying to stop the Fowlers? The Patmans, who were just as bad—a formal English garden! The whole disgusting mess was now in the courts, which only threw her father and that woman lawyer, Marianna West, together even more.

And to top it off, Todd Wilkins had turned out to be practically as bad as Rick Andover. Elizabeth couldn't stop thinking about it, and every time she did, her stomach turned. How could Todd do such a thing! At the same time, she could never quite *picture* him doing it. She believed Jessica—after all, why would she lie about such a thing?—but the image simply refused to come.

Elizabeth had never been so miserable, but she supposed it didn't matter anymore. Jessica was through with Todd—and so was she. Furthermore, Todd was waltzing around Sweet Valley High as though nothing had happened. It was obvious he didn't even care!

And yet Elizabeth was astounded to notice that Todd was watching her. Every class they had together, she could feel his eyes on her.

When they passed in the corridors, when they bumped into each other in the cafeteria, Todd tried to engage her in conversation as though they were still friends.

"Hey, Liz," he said after history one morning, "how about getting something to eat after school?"

"I'm busy," she snapped, ignoring the hurt look on Todd's face.

In Mr. Russo's class he slipped her a note: "Meet me in front of the columns after school."

Elizabeth didn't bother to keep that appointment.

But he wouldn't stop pestering her. Every day Todd tried to corner her on the stairs or stop her in the hall. She brushed him off, but it only made her feel worse.

Even when Mr. Collins came over to her desk in the *Oracle* office and praised her for the story she had done on the football field crisis, she didn't feel much better.

"That was a really professional job," Mr. Collins said.

"Thanks."

"Want to talk about it?" he asked, leaning on the edge of the desk. He had a concerned expression on his face.

Elizabeth managed to smile. "I'm sorry, Mr. Collins. Things haven't exactly been going my way lately."

"Do you think you're up to covering the rest of the football field story for *The Oracle*?"

"Of course. What's next?"

"It's a court case now. You'll have to go down to the courthouse. Your father is handling it, I know, so you'll have to be careful to remain objective."

"I will, Mr. Collins, don't worry."

"Try not to jump to any conclusions. And don't prejudice the case. You can't be a fair reporter if you do. Remember, you have to have all the facts first."

"OK."

"What's her name—Ms. West—isn't she in on this, too?"

"Yes," Elizabeth said softly. *Oh, isn't she, though!*

"All right. Be in Superior Court at nine-thirty on Tuesday, and good luck."

The thought of having to watch her father and "that woman" working together in the court-room only succeeded in making Elizabeth feel even more miserable. The telephone call the next night from Todd Wilkins did nothing to cheer her up, either.

"Liz?"

"Yes."

"It's Todd."

"What do you want!"

"Liz, something strange is going on."

"Nothing strange is going to go on between you and me, Todd Wilkins. So just get that straight."

"Would you mind making sense?" he said angrily.

"Why do you keep bothering us?"

"Us?"

"Jessica and me! Don't you realize we're not what you seem to think?"

"What are you talking about?"

"Oh, you know very well!"

"I do not!"

"Well, what do you want with me, Mr. Wilkins?"

"I've been trying to get you to meet me so I could tell you something, *Miss* Wakefield!"

"Oh?"

"I mean, well, I just wanted to tell you that I was wrong about something."

Elizabeth felt herself listening intently. If only he could explain things, she thought hopefully. If only there was a way to make things right. Even if he said he was sorry for what happened, that might help some.

"What is it, Todd?" she asked, her voice softening.

"Well, see, I just wanted to say that—well, people make mistakes. I know that. People do things without realizing it, and then they're sorry. And you can't hold it against them forever! It's not fair."

No, Elizabeth thought. That was true.

If Todd apologized for what he tried to do to Jessica, that wouldn't make it all right, exactly. But it would make her at least stop hating him some.

"I just want to apologize, Liz, for the way I've been acting."

"Well, Todd, it really did surprise me. You have no idea how shocked I was."

"Well, can you blame me, Liz? I've cooled down some now, but it took me a lot to be willing to forgive you."

Elizabeth's head spun wildly, trying to make sense of what he was saying.

"Forgive me?"

"But I do," he said hurriedly. "I forgive you on the condition that you promise not to see that creep again."

"What creep?"

"Aw, Liz, you know—Rick Andover."

"You still believe that?"

"Everybody *knows* it."

"Didn't Jessica talk to you?"

"Oh, sure. She's as loyal as the day is long, Liz. She tried to take the blame for you. It was really wonderful of her. But I want you to know it's all right. You made a mistake—it's over. I'm willing to forget about it."

"*You're* willing—?" Elizabeth felt she was going to explode. "Just forget it, Todd."

"Huh?"

"Don't do me any favors."

"Elizabeth, I'm trying to keep my cool. But this is getting to me."

"Isn't that too bad."

"Liz, listen. How about seeing me tonight? Maybe we can talk this out."

"See you tonight? You have nerve! After what you did! Todd, let's get this straight once and for all. I never want to speak to you again!"

Elizabeth slammed down the phone and cried for an hour. But at least it was finally, totally, absolutely finished. Forever!

Fifteen

The courthouse in downtown Sweet Valley was a fine, sprawling Colonial-style building. Elizabeth felt a little overwhelmed when she walked in and was directed to the press room.

"You mean reporters have their own room in the courthouse?" she asked the man in the information booth.

"Yes, young lady. Right down the hall, third door on the left."

Elizabeth walked hesitantly to the press room and peeked inside. There were large desks around the walls, most of them piled high with newspapers and stacks of official-looking court papers. A few reporters were there, too. *Maybe someday I'll work here*, Elizabeth thought.

Mr. Collins had told her to find Eric Garnet, a

reporter he knew who worked for *The Sweet Valley News*.

"Hello, Mr. Garnet," she said shyly.

"Ah, yes—the Barbara Walters of Sweet Valley High, I believe," Eric Garnet said and smiled.

Elizabeth smiled and blushed. "Not exactly."

"So, what can I do for you?"

"I'm here to cover the football field story."

"The what?"

Elizabeth felt her face reddening again. She checked her notebook. "Oh, I mean, Fowler versus the Board of Education."

He directed her to the second floor and wished her luck.

As she walked into the courtroom, Elizabeth noticed Coach Schultz and the principal, Mr. Cooper, sitting in the spectators section. Judge Robert Daly was already on the bench, wearing his black robes and looking stern and dignified.

There was George Fowler, sitting at a table with several lawyers in dark suits. He looked rather sinister and very determined. And at another table up near the judge's bench was her father and his assistant, Marianna West.

Elizabeth felt an icy stab of anger go through her at the sight of Marianna. Her father was being so attentive, leaning over with his head next to hers, whispering heaven knows what into her ear. If her mother saw that, she would die!

At a third table were Henry Wilson Patman and two more lawyers. Altogether, there were enough lawyers in the courtroom to sue everyone in the state of California.

"Are both sides ready for oral argument in this proceeding?" the judge asked, looking up from a stack of legal briefs he'd been reading.

"Ready, Your Honor," piped Marianna West before any of the others had spoken.

Elizabeth glared at Marianna West. That pushy creature didn't even let her father—a partner in the law firm—speak up; she jumped right in!

Elizabeth had little time to simmer about it, though, because one after another the lawyers started talking, throwing around long legal words that left her bewildered.

First, one of George Fowler's blue-suited lawyers got up and delivered a towering speech about how the Fowlers were entitled to the football field property because the lease held by the Sweet Valley Board of Education had lapsed and had not been renewed.

Then one of Henry Patman's lawyers got up and delivered an even more impassioned speech about how a factory would deface Sweet Valley with smoke and pollution, and insisted the public had an interest in the matter.

Elizabeth felt her spirits falling as she listened to both convincing-sounding arguments. Still, she thought, her father hadn't spoken yet. He was a wonderful lawyer. Maybe he could save the field for Sweet Valley High.

Elizabeth was stunned to see Marianna West rise to speak for the high school instead.

Marianna straightened the legal papers on the table in front of her, then began to speak. She addressed the courtroom in a clear, strong voice, arguing eloquently that the football field was "the heart" of Sweet Valley High as surely as the school building was its "mind."

Elizabeth scribbled frantically, trying to keep up with Marianna's powerful argument. She seemed to know everything about the matter, all right. Her father must have told her every detail.

Nevertheless, Elizabeth couldn't help admiring the ease with which Marianna had handled a difficult situation. She found herself writing in her notebook: "Ms. West was very impressive in marshaling the arguments for Sweet Valley High."

Elizabeth had begun to question her suspicions about Marianna West when the judge called a recess and the court retired to await his decision. She spotted her father in the corridor and rushed over to speak with him. She froze when she noticed that he had his arm slung around Marianna's shoulders. In front of everyone! What was going on?

When Ned Wakefield walked over and introduced the two of them, Elizabeth could scarcely find her voice. Fortunately, Marianna didn't notice. She was all smiles, bubbling over with her success in the courtroom. She greeted Elizabeth warmly.

"Ned told me what beautiful daughters he had," she said, "but I had no idea . . ."

Elizabeth blushed, overcome with confusion. Marianna was no phony. She was even someone Elizabeth felt she could like—a thought that made her feel traitorous toward her mother.

The bailiff stuck his head out the courtroom door and announced that the judge was back on the bench. They all filed back in and took their places. Elizabeth felt as if the entire room were holding its breath as they waited for him to announce his decision.

Amid a nearly unintelligible babble of legal jargon, the last part of what the judge was saying rang clear as a bell: "Petitions by George Fowler and Henry Patman are denied. The property shall be leased to the Sweet Valley Board of Education."

Coach Schultz, who was seated next to Chrome Dome Cooper, leaped to his feet and yelled, "Yea, Sweet Valley!"

Nobody heard the clerk calling for order in the ensuing din of cheers and excited conversation. Nobody noticed, except Elizabeth, as the Fowler and Patman entourages slunk out of the courtroom in sour-faced defeat.

Mr. Cooper and Coach Schultz drove Elizabeth back to the high school, where she was trailed down the corridors by Ken Matthews and the whole Gladiator football team.

"It's OK," she yelled. "We won!"

And then the entire backfield hoisted Elizabeth onto their shoulders and paraded her outside, down the steps, around the school, up the ramp, and through the cafeteria.

Afterward, as she wrote the story, kids kept dashing in to ask for more details.

"Did your father save us?"

"He was there, but Marianna West did the talking."

Mr. Collins read over her story and nodded approvingly. "Good, Elizabeth. Very objective."

Elizabeth sighed. She didn't feel very objective.

After school, walking home, Elizabeth sunk back into her blue mood. How could she be happy when her father was about to leave them for another woman?

When she walked in the house, her mother said, "Liz, honey, could you set the table with the good dishes and silverware? We're having guests."

"Really?"

"Yes, and I know you kids are tired of your father and me not being home for dinner. This one will be for all of us."

"That's great, Mom," Elizabeth said happily, giving her mother a hug and a kiss. "Who's coming for dinner?"

"Marianna West!" her mother said, smiling. "And—"

She didn't have a chance to say who the other guest was because Elizabeth interrupted. "Marianna West?"

"Yes! And your father has a very important announcement to make."

"An announcement about Marianna West?"

"Yes!"

Jessica hardly knew what hit her when Elizabeth dragged her into her bedroom and closed the door.

"What's the matter, Liz?"

"It's the end of the world, Jess! Marianna West is coming for dinner, and Dad's going to make an announcement. What do you think's going on?"

"I know!" cried Jessica, collapsing in tears on her bed. "They're going to announce they're getting a divorce! Oh, I could just die!"

"Oh, that's impossible. Dad would never make

that kind of announcement," Elizabeth said, but without much conviction.

"What difference does it make what he says?" sniffed Jessica. "He's in love with Marianna West, isn't he?"

"I don't know."

"Yes, you do."

The enormity of this treachery had hardly sunk in when they heard Steven come bounding up the stairs. Jessica threw open the door.

"Steve, I didn't know you were coming home tonight. Get in here! We've got a crisis! Dad's in love with Marianna West!"

"What?" said Steven, astonished.

"He's going to make an announcement at dinner," said Elizabeth. "We're not sure yet what it is, but under the circumstances, it's got to be terrible."

"Oh, no," he said, falling into a chair. "But I've invited Tricia Martin to dinner! That's why I came home tonight. We can't let her be in on this."

"This is the most horrible day in my entire existence!" Jessica raged, stomping out and heading for her room.

As the twins and Steven dressed for dinner that night, all were preparing for the worst.

Meanwhile, Alice Wakefield was busy preparing duck à l'orange, creamed asparagus, and a chilled parfait. The twins heard her humming as she worked.

"I can't stand this!" Jessica muttered.

Looking thoroughly defeated, Steven came downstairs with Elizabeth and Jessica. He hadn't been able to reach Tricia to tell her not to come. She would discover that she was not the only one whose family was a mess.

Plans to confront their father and head off the crisis didn't succeed, either, because when they got downstairs Marianna was already there, looking positively radiant in an ice-blue suit. She was sipping a glass of white wine.

Not only that. Ned and Alice Wakefield were having drinks with her, and they were all laughing and smiling together.

Then Tricia Martin came in, looking shy and uncertain.

"Hello, Tricia," Mrs. Wakefield said warmly.

"Hi, Tricia," said Ned Wakefield.

They were all being so polite and civilized the twins thought they would throw up.

And then Mr. Wakefield raised his glass. "Listen, everybody," he said. "I was going to announce this at dinner, but I just can't wait."

Elizabeth held her breath. Jessica stared daggers at her father. Steven looked as though he were going to run from the room.

"I offer a toast to Marianna," said Ned Wakefield, "the newest partner in our law firm!"

Elizabeth stared at Jessica. Jessica stared at Elizabeth.

Marianna West looked first at Ned Wakefield and then at his wife. "What?"

Mr. Wakefield laughed. "They told me I could announce it tonight, Marianna. You're a full partner as of now. All those extra hours we put in were worth something, after all."

So that's what Dad had been doing—helping Ms. West gain the promotion he thought she deserved. Elizabeth blushed, ashamed of her unfounded suspicions, while Jessica looked simply incredulous.

"Oh, my goodness!" Marianna West blurted out. "Oh, Ned, you're terrific. I couldn't have done it without your support!" She threw herself into Ned Wakefield's arms and kissed him on the cheek. Then she kissed Alice Wakefield, too.

"Alice, you have the most wonderful husband in the world."

"I know," she said, smiling and taking Ned's arm.

"Now that we've all heard the good news," said Mr. Wakefield, "why don't we adjourn— and sit down for dinner."

Elizabeth linked arms with her sister and gave her brother and Tricia a brilliant smile, as they all practically skipped to the table.

Sixteen

"I'll have a bacon cheeseburger and a root beer," Elizabeth said to the waitress before resuming her conversation with Enid. It was the next afternoon, and the girls had stopped in at the Dairi Burger after school.

"It was really something, Enid. You would have just died at the faces on Mr. Patman and Mr. Fowler! At least we don't have to worry about the football field anymore."

Suddenly Enid spotted something over Elizabeth's left shoulder.

"Let's go, Liz. I've got to get home!" Enid was on her feet, gathering up her books.

"What are you talking about, Enid? We haven't even gotten our food yet."

"I promised my mother I would clean up my room."

"You did that over the weekend. I was with you, remember?"

"Oh, yeah. Well, I have to do something else. Now!"

"Stop being weird, Enid. What's the matter with you? You look like you've just seen a ghost."

Elizabeth turned in her chair and checked out the room. Then she saw Todd and Emily Mayer sitting in a booth near the front door.

"Oh." Elizabeth turned back to face Enid, her face white and her hands shaking.

"Nice try, Enid, but I would have seen them on the way out, anyway. Don't worry. It's no big deal."

Why should the sight of Todd with another girl shake me? Elizabeth wondered. *I hate him.*

"They're probably just talking about homework assignments," Enid suggested.

"I couldn't care less what they're talking about, Enid. Todd Wilkins means nothing to me!"

"Remember me, Liz? I'm your friend. You don't have to pretend with me."

"I'm not pretending. There is nothing at all between Todd and me." *There never has been anything—and there never will be anything*, she wanted to add.

Out of the corner of her eye, she sneaked another look at Todd and Emily and wondered why it hurt so much to see him smile at the small, dark-haired girl. In addition to being The Droids' drummer, Emily was a really nice person. *I wonder if she knows what she's letting herself in for*, Elizabeth thought bitterly.

The time seemed to drag as the waitress brought their food and Elizabeth and Enid ate, exchanging only a few words. Finally they could leave.

Elizabeth held her head high and wore her brightest smile as she and Enid approached the front of Dairi Burger.

"Hi, Emily. Hey, The Droids were terrific at the dance. You guys are really something else!"

"Thanks, Liz," said Emily.

"Hello, Liz."

"Hi, Todd. See you two around."

Elizabeth walked as fast as she could out the door, through the parking lot, and to the car. There was only one thought in her head: *don't let me cry, don't let me make a fool of myself!*

Seventeen

Of course Elizabeth had heard people say before that they didn't really feel the pain of being
hurt until afterward, but she had never believed
it before. The time she got her thumb stuck in
the door and the time she hit her shin on the
kitchen chair, there was no doubt about it. Both
had hurt right away, and plenty. But Elizabeth
didn't really feel the pain of losing Todd for
several days after seeing him with Emily. And
then she wished for that other kind of pain, the
kind that came at once and went away almost
as quickly. Because this pain sat in her heart as
though it were a bird that had built its nest
there and would never go away. She had known
it was over, really. It had never even started.
But seeing him with someone else—that made
it final as nothing else could have.

She decided to go on other dates, too. She couldn't just think about Todd forever. She went skating with Ken Matthews one Friday night when the team went out together. It wasn't a real date, though. Just a celebration of getting the football field back. Still, Ken picked her up and brought her home, under the watchful eye of Jessica. It seemed Jessica thought Ken still had a girlfriend, and if she had known he didn't . . .

After that, Elizabeth told herself she was over Todd for good and she would absolutely stop thinking about him all the time. But she thought about practically nothing else.

One night after a sorority meeting at Caroline Pearce's house—at which Elizabeth totally ignored Caroline, still angry at her for spreading the rumors about Kelly's—they all trooped to the Dairi Burger for hamburgers, and there were Todd and all the Phi Eps. Elizabeth tried not to look at Todd, and she could tell he was doing the same. *Why is he acting this way?* she asked herself. It was over. He never called her anymore. They avoided each other in the halls. Still, Todd was being careful not to look at her, and she was being just as careful not to look at him.

After their burgers, they climbed into the Fiat convertible—Jessica was allowed to drive again—

and off they went with three of their friends in the car.

They dropped off Enid and Cara first. When they dropped off Lila Fowler, Elizabeth noticed that they were being followed.

"Oh, don't be silly," said Jessica.

"I tell you, there's a car on our tail, Jess."

They both noticed it after that. A sleek black sports car trailed them as they drove, and it was getting closer and closer.

"Oh, Liz," Jessica gasped. "I'm scared."

"Never mind. Just head straight for home."

But Jessica managed to stall the Fiat at the next red light, and then, in her anxiety, she couldn't get it started again. The pursuing car pulled over to the curb behind them. The driver got out, walked up, and leaned over the side to leer at them.

"Well, well, well. If it isn't Heaven and her sister, Heavenly."

Jessica exploded. "Rick Andover, you scared me to death! I didn't recognize you without your car."

"Aw, sorry," he said mockingly. "Mine's in the shop. I borrowed that little number. You like it? Or would you rather I took you for a ride in this one?"

"Jessie," Elizabeth whispered. "He's drunk."

"Now, is that nice?" Rick sneered. "I heard

you, Heavenly. And you're a smart girl. I *am* drunk, but not enough to matter. Look out!"

And before Jessica could stop him, Rick Andover pulled open the door and jumped into the driver's seat, squeezing her over next to Elizabeth.

"What are you doing?" Jessica raged. "You get out of this car!"

"Got to start it for you, Heaven," Rick slurred. "Can't let you sit here in the middle of Calico Drive."

"Well, start it and then get out," Elizabeth said.

As if on cue, the Spider's engine leaped to life. But Rick Andover did not get out. He floored the gas pedal, and the little red Fiat screeched down the drive as if it were in the Indianapolis 500.

"Stop!" Jessica screamed. "Stop this car!"

"You let us out!" Elizabeth shouted.

Rick Andover laughed drunkenly, stomping down harder on the gas pedal. The Fiat zoomed wildly, looping around toward the Dairi Burger on the bottom of the hill.

They careened past the Dairi Burger, and Elizabeth yelled out the window.

"Help! Somebody!"

Rick whipped the little car through the crowded parking lot of the Dairi Burger, swerving at the last second to miss a crowd of Sweet Valley kids coming out.

Elizabeth caught a fleeting glance of a face startled and pulling back with sudden fright. Todd Wilkins!

Again the Fiat screeched around the parking lot, scattering people with terrifying bursts of speed and last-minute sharp turns.

"Out of the way, you idiots!" Rick Andover yelled. "We're coming through!"

Rick zipped the little car backward, spun around, and tore out of the Dairi Burger lot, almost sideswiping one car and rear-ending another. The car plunged into the traffic and sped wildly off in the direction of the beach.

Looking back, the last thing Elizabeth saw was Todd Wilkins standing near the front door, looking after them in bewilderment.

But Todd's bewilderment vanished the instant he saw the terror on Elizabeth's face and turned to sheer fury at the sight of Rick Andover at the wheel. Within seconds, he had jumped into his Datsun and was speeding after them.

The red Fiat zipped in and out of traffic on the freeway, passing cars and trucks on the inside or the outside as the whim struck Rick.

Jessica's contorted face was wet with tears. "Make him stop," she begged Elizabeth.

"Rick, you stop this car, or I'll—" Elizabeth commanded.

Rick uttered a harsh bark of laughter. "Scream as loud as you like. Who's going to hear you?"

Elizabeth shot Jessica a terrified look. Rick was really crazy. He could wind up killing them!

"Oh, no!" Jessica wailed as he made a screeching turn down a familiar road. "He's taking us to Kelly's!"

"I'll show that creep," he was muttering. "Nobody shows Rick Andover the door if he knows what's good for him."

"They'll never believe we're not with him," Jessica hissed to her sister. "They'll really arrest us this time."

Rick's only response was to hit the gas pedal harder. He didn't notice that a battered old Datsun was slowly gaining on them. Finally, with a screaming skid, Rick spun the Fiat around the parking lot of Kelly's in a boiling cloud of dust and sand. He grabbed Jessica with one hand and Elizabeth with the other, yanking them out of the car. He cursed loudly as the Datsun jerked to a stop in front of him, blocking the entrance to the roadhouse.

"Hey, get that heap out of the way!" he yelled.

Todd Wilkins climbed from the Datsun, a tough look on his face, a look that meant business.

"Todd!" the twins screamed in unison.

"Get back in the car," Todd commanded them soberly as Rick released them to advance on this new menace. Rick's fists were knotted at his sides, and there was a murderous look in his eye.

"Who are you to give orders?" growled Rick. "Get out of my way before I teach you a lesson."

"The only one going anyplace is you, Rick," said Todd quietly. "Why don't you just go home and sleep it off, huh?"

Rick's fist caught Todd square on the jaw in a lightning punch that took him completely off guard. Todd jerked backward but didn't fall. Elizabeth gasped when she saw his nose was bleeding. But after that first stunned pause, Todd didn't miss a beat. He came to life in a fury of hard, short jabs to the middle that sent Rick jackknifing to his knees, clutching at his stomach and gasping for breath.

Todd turned to Elizabeth and Jessica. "Come on. I think he'll leave you alone now. It doesn't look as if he'll be bothering anyone for a while."

"Are you all right?" Elizabeth brought a trembling hand to Todd's face.

Todd smiled. "Sure—as long as nothing's broken. Are *you* OK?"

Elizabeth nodded.

"I thought he was going to kill you!" Jessica gushed. "Oh, Todd, you were wonderful! You practically saved our lives!" She glared in the direction of Rick and the roadhouse. "I never want to see this place again. It's even worse inside."

Todd gave her a funny look but said nothing.

"I could just kiss you!" Jessica squealed, rushing toward him.

She was intercepted as Elizabeth stepped in front of her. "Not this time, Jess. It's my turn." With that, she turned to kiss a surprised Todd squarely on the mouth.

It wasn't until the Fiat was back at the Wakefields' house and he was parked in front that Todd confronted Jessica.

"Hey, Jessica," he said. "What did you mean when you said you never wanted to see Kelly's Roadhouse *again*?"

"Well, I don't, Todd."

"But how do *you* know how rough it is in there?"

"I really am simply too worn out to go on with this," Jessica said suddenly, looking from Todd to Elizabeth. "Good night!"

And before either of them could say another word, Jessica had skipped into the house.

"Hey—"

"Todd, thank you so much. You saved our lives," Elizabeth said. "I didn't know what we were going to do."

"Liz, do you mean that—that other time—it really wasn't you?"

Elizabeth only looked at him.

"But—"

"Todd, didn't Jessica tell you it was her?"

"Well, yes. But—"

"But what?"

"That's really amazing. She said it was her, but—Liz, I'm so sorry. I should have known you wouldn't have—that you never could have. . . . How could I have been such an idiot?"

"You weren't alone, Todd. Everybody thought it was me—especially when *somebody* has a funny way of telling the truth." *Somebody who bears a striking resemblance to me*, she thought.

"I was such a fool," Todd was saying. "But you were so popular, with dates every night. I guess I thought anything was possible. You never would give me a look."

"What? Todd, who told you such insane things?"

"Jessica."

"*Jessica?*"

"Well, yes. She constantly told me how popular you were and that you had no time for me. Well, I could see it was true."

"I see. And that's why you decided to go after Jessica?"

"Go after Jessica? One date? And I tell you, I'm not quite sure how that even happened."

"Is that so? How's your memory on what happened at the *end* of that date when she had to beg you to stop—grabbing her?"

167

"When she had to do what? Who told you that?"

"Jessica!"

"Liz, I barely touched Jessica. I gave her a little peck on the cheek at the door—and I only did that 'cause she seemed to expect it!"

"What?"

"Yes! Liz, you're the only one I ever wanted. Not Jessica, not anybody."

Todd was moving closer to her.

"But what about Emily?"

"Emily Mayer? We have a history project together."

"You didn't touch Jessica?"

"No. You didn't go out with Rick?"

"Absolutely not!"

Todd shook his head in confusion. How could it all have happened? It was impossible.

Elizabeth smiled to herself, trying to picture the hilarious scene of Todd kissing Jessica on the cheek. Why, she must have been ready to burst into a million pieces!

Seeing her smile, Todd asked, "What's funny?"

"Nothing," Elizabeth said.

Whatever she was going to say next was lost forever because suddenly she was in Todd's arms, and they were locked in a long and searching kiss. Elizabeth felt her heart pounding and her ears ringing, and she found herself wishing the moment would last forever.

Todd's breath was warm against her ear. "There's never been anyone but you, Liz," he murmured.

"Only someone who *pretended* she was me." Elizabeth laughed softly, pulling Todd closer for another, longer kiss that was sweeter than anything she had imagined.

Eighteen

Elizabeth floated through the living room and up the stairs to her room. She headed straight for the mirror and smiled at what she saw reflected there.

Yes, that was most definitely the face of a person in love. What was even better, she thought, was that it was the face of a person who was loved in return.

She hurriedly got out of her clothes and slipped on her nightshirt. She could hardly wait to get to bed. Her dreams were bound to be terrific that night.

Wait, she reminded herself. There was one little thing that had to be done—immediately.

Elizabeth marched through the bathroom and into her sister's room.

"Jess," she said, "we have to talk."

Jessica was fussing with her new eye makeup.

"If I use this aqua liner, it makes my eyes look greener. What do you think?" Jessica asked, sticking her face right into Elizabeth's.

"I think it won't work."

"You like blue better?"

"Come on, Jess. You know what I'm talking about."

"Honestly, I don't," Jessica said, her eyes indeed looking almost pure green and very innocent. "If something's wrong, tell me."

"You bet I will."

"You know I'd do anything to help you, Lizzie," she said. "After all, you're the closest person in the whole world to me."

"Jessica."

"There's no one who means more."

"Todd told me everything."

"And you believe him over your own sister," she said, switching gears without missing a beat.

Elizabeth plowed on, paying no attention to the crushed look on Jessica's face. "He said he never tried to kiss you or anything else."

"Is that all?" She brightened. That was an easy one for a pro like Jessica.

"No. There's lots more."

"Like what?" Trouble again.

"Like your visit to Kelly's with Rick Andover."

"I've already explained that. Besides, it's ancient history. As for Todd trying to paw me, well, it's true that he didn't, but I only told you he did for your own benefit."

"Oh, come on!"

"No, really, I thought I was helping you."

"Just how did it help me to think that the guy I liked was after my sister?"

"Lizzie, honey. I did it because I felt he was wrong for you. That you wouldn't be able to handle him."

"Jessie, *honey*. You're really full of it. You did it because you liked him yourself and you were trying to get rid of the competition."

Jessica, seeing that she was cornered, tried a different tack. "You're right," she confessed. "I guess I did like Todd a little. But, honestly, I didn't realize he was so important to you. Besides, it all turned out OK because he really does like you. He certainly showed it tonight. He's a terrific person, and I'm really happy for both of you."

"Jess, you were spying on us just now," Elizabeth accused.

"Come on, Liz. I said I was sorry. Can't we just forget it? After all, you make mistakes, too."

"What about Kelly's?"

"I've told you and *told* you about that. Jeez, Liz, I can't talk anymore. I've got to get to bed. My head is bursting. I must be coming down with something. Here, feel my forehead." She leaned over to her sister, her face pale with instant terminal illness.

Elizabeth ignored the extended forehead. Instead, she took Jessica by the shoulders and moved her back so that they were eye to eye. "Tell me one more time, Jessie."

"It was ages ago. Let's forget it."

"I mean it, Jessica."

Elizabeth was only four minutes older than Jessica, but in a pinch she could make those minutes really count. Like now. Elizabeth was in charge, and there was no way out for Jessica— who knew it. She burst into tears.

"How could you let everybody think I was at Kelly's?" she demanded of the sobbing Jessica. "How could you do such a horrendous thing to me?"

"I'm sorry, honestly, I swear I am. Forgive me." Jessica's pleading face was drenched in tears. "Even when it was happening, I knew it was a horrible thing to do."

"I never would have done such a thing to you."

"I know you wouldn't, and that's what makes it so awful. But I just couldn't help myself."

"Why not?"

"Because . . ." She started but couldn't go on. Her sobs turned everything into an unintelligible babble of how she was so ashamed of herself for being so selfish and awful and on and on. But Elizabeth was determined. She was not going to accept any apologies until Jessica made a full confession.

Finally Jessica, exhausting all her self-recriminations, saw that she had to tell Elizabeth the real reason.

"I knew if it got around school that I was in that bar with those terrible people, I'd be finished. It's a rule, an absolute rule, that you can't be on the cheering squad if you have any black marks against your name. I couldn't give that up, Liz. You know how much being co-captain of the cheerleaders means to me."

"What about me? Didn't you care if I got into trouble for something I didn't even do?"

"But you wouldn't have—and you didn't! You're not a cheerleader, and I knew they wouldn't kick you off the newspaper. Sure, some dumb kids gossiped about you, but so what? They do that, anyway. Still, I knew nothing really bad would happen to you, but it would have been the end of everything for me. I couldn't bear it. Besides, Liz, I know you would have helped if I asked you. Wouldn't you have?"

"I don't know."

"If you knew how much it meant to me?"

"I guess so."

"You know you would have." She sniffled. "But I couldn't ask you. It all happened too fast." Now the tears came again. "You know you're the most important person in the world to me. I'll die if you don't forgive me. Please, Lizzie."

This time the affection was sincere, and Elizabeth was won over.

"I can't ever stay angry with you," she said, and before she had a chance to say another word, Jessica threw her arms around her with such emotion that poor Elizabeth squealed.

Elizabeth hugged her back. No matter what happened between them, this mirror image, this other half of herself, would always be connected to her in some strange and powerful way. And that relationship would be different and separate from any other she would ever have in her life. Nothing could ever change that. Not for either of them.

Jessica's face was shining with pleasure and relief. She really couldn't bear to have her sister angry with her. Elizabeth knew that, and only wanted to see Jessica happy. And happy she was—for the moment.

But Elizabeth had a score to settle with Jessica, and she knew exactly how she was going to do it. She didn't intend to tell anyone but Todd— since he was a part of her fantastic plan.

Nineteen

Elizabeth checked herself in the mirror one last time. "Looking good, Liz," she told herself, twisting around to see if her tuxedo shirt was tucked in neatly at the back.

She was finally going to have a chance to wear her new outfit, and she couldn't have chosen a better time.

Now for the next step in her plan.

"Jess, are you almost ready?" she called. "Todd will be here to pick us up in a few minutes."

"I don't see why I have to ride to the rally with you and Todd," Jessica grumbled as she came into the room. "I could have driven the Spider."

"Not without the keys, and I guess Mom forgot to leave them." Elizabeth crossed her fingers behind her back.

"You and Todd will be crawling all over each other right in front of me!"

"I promise not to embarrass you, Jess. Maybe we'll do a little hand-holding." *Maybe a lot of hand-holding.*

Now for step three.

Elizabeth picked up the glass of water that was on her dresser, and somehow it spilled all over Jessica's white blouse and blue miniskirt.

"How could you be so clumsy?" *Look what you've done!*

"Oh, Jess, I'm sorry. I don't know how in the world I could have done such a thing. Let me help you dry it off."

"There isn't time! Now what am I going to wear? There isn't another clean outfit in my closet." Jessica moaned.

"Well, since it was my fault," Elizabeth said, guilt and a spark of something else radiating from her eyes, "it's up to me to solve your problem."

"How?"

"I just pressed my best jeans today and my blue button-down shirt that you've been dying to borrow."

Jessica was stunned. "You're serious? You'd let me borrow that outfit?"

"Yes, but just this once."

Jessica made a quick change, then stood admiring her image in the mirror.

"Look at us, Liz. Do you see something funny?"

"No. You look terrific."

"I don't mean that, silly. Look again. If I didn't know which of us was me, I would swear you were me and I was you."

It took all of Elizabeth's ample supply of self-control to keep from bursting into laughter. It was like taking candy from a baby.

"You know, you're right, Jess. You look just like me."

"What is that horrendous noise?"

"It's just Todd's car. He's having a little muffler trouble. Let's go. I don't want to keep him waiting."

The two girls dashed out to Todd. Jessica missed the conspiratorial wink Elizabeth and Todd exchanged because she was too busy complaining about being seen in such a gross car.

By the time they drove to school, parked the car, and walked over to where the crowd was gathered, Elizabeth was ready to put step four of her plan into action.

The Droids were entertaining the crowd before the football rally started, and Dana Larson was belting out a number in true Droid fashion.

"Excuse me a minute, you guys. I have to see Dana about an article on the Droids. I'm going to try and catch her at the end of this number. Be right back." She hurried off into the crowd.

"I've got to go, too, Todd. I want to talk to Lila and Cara." She started off, but Todd grabbed her arm.

"Don't tell me you're deserting me, too, Jess. You can't leave me here all alone, friendless and unwanted," Todd teased with mock sadness. Then he gave Jessica his most charming grin.

"Oh, don't be silly, Todd. You know practically every single person here." She smiled up at him, the flirt in her unable to resist a good-looking guy's smile. She sighed. "You're a nut, Todd, but I'll stay until Liz gets back."

"Thanks, Jess. That will make Liz happy." *I'll say it'll make her happy*, he thought, smiling to himself.

Elizabeth made it over to the bandstand just as Dana finished her number and stepped down to the ground.

"Hey, Jess," Dana said, snapping her gum, "every time you wear that tuxedo outfit, you make the other fashion types around here look like they're wearing horse blankets."

"Thanks, Dana. It really is *me*, isn't it?" Elizabeth said, flashing a truly glorious Jessica Wakefield smile.

"Sure thing, Jess."

Elizabeth grinned to herself. It was working!

"Dana, I have the *most* sensational announcement for you to make about the 'Eyes and Ears' column."

It was a tradition that, every year, if the "Eyes and Ears" author was unmasked, the guilty party was thrown, fully clothed, into the school pool. Elizabeth couldn't remember any previous columnist escaping the students' playful punishment. Somebody always leaked the secret, at just about this point in the semester. Elizabeth suspected it was Mr. Collins and that her time was almost up. Well, this year, somebody else was going to spill the beans.

"I know who writes the column," Elizabeth said, imitating Jessica perfectly.

"Terrific, Jess. We have time for a little dunking before the rally starts. Who is it?"

"My sister. Liz is the author."

"And you're turning her in? What's the matter, you two have a fight?"

"No, no. It's just that sometimes she seems a little *too* good, you know? A little dunking won't hurt her."

"You're right. Besides, she's a good sport. Where is she?"

"Where else? Over there with Todd Wilkins, where she *always* is."

"OK! Let's tell the world the news." Dana jumped back onto the bandstand, grabbed the mike, and held up her hand for attention.

"Listen up, you guys! Have I got news for

you! What do we do to the writer of the 'Eyes and Ears' column?"

"Dunk him!" the crowd roared.

"Well, go get *her*. It's Liz Wakefield—and she's standing right over there with Todd Wilkins!"

Everyone turned to look. Jessica stood rooted to the ground. "Oh, no, Todd, they think I'm Liz. Help me, Todd. Stop them!"

Smiling broadly, Todd stepped away from her.

"Rules are rules, *Liz*. She's all yours, guys."

Two linebackers got to her first. One took her arms, the other her legs. They headed for the pool, followed by a laughing crowd.

"No! No! No! I'm not Liz, you jerks! I'm Jessica!"

One of the guys laughed. "Give me a break, Liz. I saw your sexy sister talking to Dana at the bandstand. I think she's the one who turned you in."

"One! Two! Three!" Jessica was thrown screaming into the middle of the pool.

Elizabeth made it down to Todd's side at the pool in time to see a sputtering, incensed, and very wet Jessica surface.

Elizabeth grinned down at her sister triumphantly. "You were right, Jessie. You certainly did look like me today."

"You planned this!" she shrieked. "You planned this whole rotten, mean, contemptible trick! I'll never forgive you, not if I live to be a hundred and thirty-seven years—"

"Bye, Jess." Elizabeth and Todd strolled off, arm in arm.

After the rally, Elizabeth and Todd finally said good night—a long good night filled with kisses and sweet words, and still more kisses.

Elizabeth watched Todd drive off, then went in, closed the door, and leaned against it, sighing happily.

The sharp ring of the doorbell announced Enid's arrival. Elizabeth had invited her friend to come over after dinner and spend the night. Elizabeth opened the door. There stood her friend, tears streaming down her face.

"Enid! What's wrong?"

"Liz, I don't know what to do. Something terrible has happened. I can't even tell you, it's so awful. But I know Ronnie is going to hate me, and I could just die! I'm afraid I'm going to lose everything."

What is the dark mystery in Enid's past, and how does Jessica use it to her own advantage? Find out in Sweet Valley High #2, SECRETS.

☐	26741	**DOUBLE LOVE #1**	$2.75
☐	26621	**SECRETS #2**	$2.75
☐	26627	**PLAYING WITH FIRE #3**	$2.75
☐	26746	**POWER PLAY #4**	$2.75
☐	26742	**ALL NIGHT LONG #5**	$2.75
☐	26813	**DANGEROUS LOVE #6**	$2.75
☐	26622	**DEAR SISTER #7**	$2.75
☐	26744	**HEARTBREAKER #8**	$2.75
☐	26626	**RACING HEARTS #9**	$2.75
☐	26620	**WRONG KIND OF GIRL #10**	$2.75
☐	26824	**TOO GOOD TO BE TRUE #11**	$2.75
☐	26688	**WHEN LOVE DIES #12**	$2.75
☐	26619	**KIDNAPPED #13**	$2.75
☐	26764	**DECEPTIONS #14**	$2.75
☐	26765	**PROMISES #15**	$2.75
☐	26740	**RAGS TO RICHES #16**	$2.75
☐	24723	**LOVE LETTERS #17**	$2.50
☐	26687	**HEAD OVER HEELS #18**	$2.75
☐	26823	**SHOWDOWN #19**	$2.75
☐	24947	**CRASH LANDING! #20**	$2.50

Prices and availability subject to change without notice.

Buy them at your local bookstore or use this convenient coupon for ordering:

SWEET DREAMS are fresh, fun and exciting—alive with the flavor of the contemporary teen scene—the joy and doubt of *first love*. If you've missed any SWEET DREAMS titles, from #1 to #100, then you're missing out on *your* kind of stories, written about people like *you!*

☐ 24460	**P.S. I LOVE YOU #1** Barbara P. Conklin	**$2.25**
☐ 24332	**THE POPULARITY PLAN #2** Rosemary Vernon	**$2.25**
☐ 24318	**LAURIE'S SONG #3** Debra Brand	**$2.25**
☐ 26613	**LITTLE SISTER #5** Yvonne Green	**$2.50**
☐ 24323	**COVER GIRL #9** Yvonne Green	**$2.25**
☐ 24324	**LOVE MATCH #10** Janet Quin-Harkin	**$2.25**
☐ 24832	**NIGHT OF THE PROM #12** Debra Spector	**$2.25**
☐ 24291	**TEN-BOY SUMMER #18** Janet Quin-Harkin	**$2.25**
☐ 26614	**THE POPULARITY SUMMER #20** Rosemary Vernon	**$2.50**
☐ 24338	**SUMMER DREAMS #36** Barbara Conklin	**$2.25**
☐ 24838	**THE TRUTH ABOUT ME AND BOBBY V. #41** Janetta Johns	**$2.25**
☐ 24688	**SECRET ADMIRER #81** Debra Spector	**$2.25**
☐ 24383	**HEY, GOOD LOOKING #82** Jane Polcovar	**$2.25**
☐ 24823	**LOVE BY THE BOOK #83** Anne Park	**$2.25**
☐ 24718	**THE LAST WORD #84** Susan Blake	**$2.25**
☐ 24890	**THE BOY SHE LEFT BEHIND #85** Suzanne Rand	**$2.25**
☐ 24945	**QUESTIONS OF LOVE #86** Rosemary Vernon	**$2.25**
☐ 24824	**PROGRAMMED FOR LOVE #87** Marion Crane	**$2.25**
☐ 24891	**WRONG KIND OF BOY #88** Shannon Blair	**$2.25**
☐ 24946	**101 WAYS TO MEET MR. RIGHT #89** Janet Quin-Harkin	**$2.25**
☐ 24992	**TWO'S A CROWD #90** Diana Gregory	**$2.25**
☐ 25070	**THE LOVE HUNT #91** Yvonne Green	**$2.25**

☐ 26843	KISS & TELL #92 Janet Quin-Harkin	$2.50
☐ 26743	THE GREAT BOY CHASE #93 Janet Quin-Harkin	$2.50
☐ 25132	SECOND CHANCES #94 Nany Levinso	$2.25
☐ 25178	NO STRINGS ATTACHED #95 Eileen Hehl	$2.25
☐ 25179	FIRST, LAST, AND ALWAYS #96 Barbara Conklin	$2.25
☐ 25244	DANCING IN THE DARK #97 Carolyn Ross	$2.25
☐ 25245	LOVE IS IN THE AIR #98 Diana Gregory	$2.25
☐ 25297	ONE BOY TOO MANY #99 Marian Caudell	$2.25
☐ 26747	FOLLOW THAT BOY #100 Debra Spector	$2.50
☐ 25366	WRONG FOR EACH OTHER #101 Debra Spector	$2.25 ·
☐ 25367	HEARTS DON'T LIE #102 Terri Fields	$2.25
☐ 25429	CROSS MY HEART #103 Diana Gregory	$2.25
☐ 25428	PLAYING FOR KEEPS #104 Janice Stevens	$2.25
☐ 25469	THE PERFECT BOY #105 Elizabeth Reynolds	$2.25
☐ 25470	MISSION: LOVE #106 Kathryn Maris	$2.25
☐ 25535	IF YOU LOVE ME #107 Barbara Steiner	$2.25
☐ 25536	ONE OF THE BOYS #108 Jill Jarnow	$2.25
☐ 25643	NO MORE BOYS #109 White	$2.25
☐ 25642	PLAYING GAMES #110 Eileen Hehl	$2.25
☐ 25726	STOLEN KISSES #111 Elizabeth Reynolds	$2.50
☐ 25727	LISTEN TO YOUR HEART #112 Marian Caudell	$2.50
☐ 25814	PRIVATE EYES #113 Julia Winfield	$2.50
☐ 25815	JUST THE WAY YOU ARE #114 Janice Boies	$2.50

Prices and availability subject to change without notice.

Special Offer
Buy a Bantam Book
for only 50¢.

Now you can order the exciting books you've been
wanting to read straight from Bantam's latest
listing of hundreds of titles. *And* this special offer
gives you the opportunity to purchase a Bantam
book for only 50¢. Here's how:

By ordering any five books at the regular price
per order, you can also choose any other single
book listed (up to $4.95 value) for only 50¢. Some
restrictions do apply, so for further details send
for Bantam's listing of titles today.

Just send us your name and address and we'll send
you Bantam Book's SHOP AT HOME CATALOG!

BANTAM BOOKS, INC.
P.O. Box 1006, South Holland, ILL. 60473

Mr./Mrs./Miss/Ms._____
                    (please print)

Address _____

City_____ State _____ Zip _____

FC(B)—11/85

Printed in the U.S.A.